His Model Student

Getting involved with him probably would be playing with fire.

But she wanted to be burned...

Briefly she closed her eyes, only to be startled by a sharp command. "Don't fall asleep!"

As if she could do that. Lying at a weird angle on the couch without moving was hardly comfortable, even if it was a very large and spacious couch.

"I'm wide awake."

"Good, because you wouldn't enjoy my method of waking you up." His gaze seared into hers for a moment and she was tempted to try it, to test him. To pretend to doze off so he would be forced to come and wake her. Maybe with a kiss, Sleeping Beauty style?

"It involves cold water," Mr Marek said, disillusioning her. Sera hoped he hadn't read her mind.

"You could just call out," she said.

He gave a taunting smile. "Cold water has other advantages."

"Such as?"

"It perks things up, should they need it." His eyes ran along her body suggestively.

"They won't need it," Sera told him, trying to maintain her composure.

"So I can see."

HIS MODEL STUDENT

by

Noël Cades

First Printing, 2016

ISBN: 0-9945811-3-0
ISBN-13: 978-0-9945811-3-6

This book is dedicated to Linda

When I look up from painting, eyes tired out,
The walls become illumined, brick from brick
Distinct, instead of mortar, fierce bright gold,
That gold of his I did cement them with!
Let us but love each other.

Andrea del Sarto - Robert Browning

1. Evening class

"Get undressed and hurry up about it. Immediately. You've already kept us waiting." Steel-dark eyes glowered into hers.

Taken aback, Sera struggled to speak. "But..."

"I don't want any excuses. You're late enough as it is."

"But I'm not..."

"Either get your clothes off and get on that couch, or you can leave and not come back."

"If I could just..."

"Now!"

Afterwards, Sera was never quite sure why she complied. It was partly because she was so shocked and embarrassed by the whole situation and intimidated by the man's furious, commanding voice.

It was also because she felt pretty angry herself: he refused to even give a chance to explain herself. If she obeyed his order, he would end up being forced to make a humiliating apology.

And - although she couldn't quite admit it to herself - he was devastatingly attractive. Tall and broad shouldered, with black, tousled hair and a chiselled jaw, he looked nothing like the "Miss E Fotheringay" who was supposed to be taking Life Drawing Course No 46 at Edenvale Community Art Centre.

Who the hell was he? And why was he so angry?

Taking off her clothes seemed like the only weapon she had. If nothing else, it would be a good lesson in empathy for the models she was going to be painting over the next few weeks. Sera had often wondered what it must be like for them: stuck in awkward positions for hours on end, naked and scrutinised by a roomful of people.

She hurriedly pulled her clothes off behind the screen. She wasn't the world's most confident person when it came to her body: she would have preferred slightly fewer curves and a couple of inches extra height. But this was an art class, not a fashion catwalk, and she knew that life models ranged widely in age, size and shape.

It was only as Sera slipped on a thin silk kimono, conveniently hung over the top, that she realised she was about to be stark naked for the first time before a roomful of strangers. They had blurred into the background during the angry confrontation. If only her hair, strawberry blonde and wavy, was as long as Botticelli's Venus it could have covered her modesty.

Still, she had started this adventure now and she wasn't going to chicken out.

"Finally. You can recline there, like so." The tall man briefly showed her a painting in an art book: she was to copy a famous pose.

Sera looked around at the other artists as she took her place. It was a small class and there were only five other students. They included two women and three men. An elderly woman with snow-white hair and twinkling eyes sat on the left in a mauve smock, next to her was a bald man with glasses and a beard. A woman with a lot of frizzy hair, playing rather anxiously with her dangling jewellery, sat in the middle. Two elderly men, one of whom wore a purple silk cravat, were on the right.

Fortunately none of them looked like perverts. Most seemed more interested in adjusting their easels and getting out painting equipment than ogling her.

Sera felt like an object but in a way it was comforting. No one was looking at her as a person, just as an abstract shape. There was no appreciation in anyone's gaze, nothing sexual. The elderly man in the cravat held up his paintbrush in the air and squinted with one eye, trying to get the right proportions.

Even the teacher seemed dispassionate. "A few inches this way. Rest your leg there. Your arm straighter, along the back of the couch." Sera flinched momentarily as his fingers touched the skin of her arm. His touch burned.

He was so close she could feel the heat and maleness of him: the fresh linen of his shirt, a trace of aromatic cologne.

Eventually he was satisfied and addressed the class. "We'll use this pose for a fifteen minute warm up, then we'll change."

Sera may as well have been a vase of flowers or a bowl of fruit.

About ten minutes later, when she was already starting to feel cramp in one leg, the door burst open. A thin girl with bright red hennaed hair burst in.

"I'm so sorry. There was an accident on the highway and I was stuck between a car and truck for half an hour. Am I too late? I can get ready very quickly." She saw Sera on the couch. "Oh..."

The art teacher had frozen. He looked at the girl and back at Sera.

"Exactly who is the model for this class?" His tone was icy.

"I am," the girl said. "Unless you've found a replacement?"

The teacher looked at Sera and in that instant his gaze changed. Suddenly she was no longer a professional model but a flesh-and-blood female, lying naked before him. Recognition flickered in his eyes as his gaze swept her naked curves. For a moment he drank in her form, then concealed his reaction as quickly as it had appeared.

Sera gave a half smile. "I'm actually one of the students."

He was silent for a moment, a muscle twitching in his jaw. The others in the room had put their pencils and charcoal down, enthralled by the unfolding drama.

"It seems I owe you an apology." He sounded far more furious than sorry. "I'm not sure why you felt obliged to model for us."

The cravat man was suppressing a chuckle and even the elderly lady was looking amused.

"I did try to explain."

The teacher gritted his teeth. "You can rejoin the class." He checked a sheet of paper and turned to the new girl. "I assume you are actually Kirsten Prout and not an art student?"

"That's right. It's usually Miss Fotheringay on Thursday nights," the model pointed out.

"I'll be taking her classes this term." He offered no explanation as to why.

The frizzy haired woman looked worried. "Is Elsie alright?"

"I wouldn't know."

He was in the foulest mood, Sera thought, but it was all his own fault. She noticed how a strand of hair kept falling over his forehead and he pushed it back, irritated. His hair needed a cut. It wasn't an intentionally long style but an overgrown short one.

He had high cheekbones and there was something almost Slavic about his features, though his voice was entirely English, clipped and correct. Sera found herself longing to sketch his portrait.

But she turned her attention to the model they were supposed to be drawing. Compared to the other students who seemed like old hands at this, Sera was a total beginner.

Glancing around she saw that most people seemed to concentrate on the limbs and the angle of the pose, rather than details such as the face. So although she enjoyed sketching faces most of all, she did likewise and focused on the figure and form.

She was painfully conscious whenever the teacher passed by her easel, feeling sure he must be wincing at her amateur attempt. It took a lot of effort just to keep her hand steady.

* * *

"Anyone for the pub? I think we could all do with wetting our whistle," the man in the purple cravat suggested as they walked out into the car park. His name turned out to be Jasper. "You more so than any of us, after that wonderful performance," he said to Sera.

Sera, who had planned on catching the bus, blushed. "It wasn't quite what I was expecting," she said.

"It was absolutely marvellous, wasn't it Barry? Certainly more dramatic than any of dear Elsie's classes."

The elderly lady and the bearded man politely declined the invitation to the pub and went their separate ways. That left Sera, the frizzy-haired woman whose name was Elizabeth, Jasper and Barry.

They went to the Norfolk Arms which was just across the road from the community centre. It was the kind of quiet pub that didn't bother to check ID, fake or otherwise, to Sera's relief. At this hour on a Thursday night it was relatively quiet.

Jasper insisted on buying the first round so Sera chose a vodka and coke.

"Thanks."

"We must thank you, for putting that arrogant if very talented young man in his place." It was true that the teacher seemed incredibly talented. He had been able to glance at their sketches and immediately suggest adjustments to restore the correct proportions. His manner with Sera had been formal to the point of cold, but she was so embarrassed after the initial adrenalin of the confrontation had worn off that she was only too happy for him to keep his distance.

Also, every time he had stood near her easel, she had been so disturbed by his presence that it was hard to keep her hand steady.

"He was terribly rude to you, I wouldn't have known what to do with myself in your place," Elizabeth said. "I certainly don't imagine he was expecting things to turn out quite as they did."

"I imagine a boy with his looks rarely gets refused anything," Jasper said. "Wouldn't you say so, Barry?"

Sera was amused to hear him call their art teacher a boy. He had seemed very much a man: he looked at least thirty.

"Indeed," Barry said.

Sera wondered if the two elderly gents were a couple or merely friends. They clearly knew one another very well. Jasper was the more flamboyant and outspoken of the two: she wasn't surprised to learn that he was a retired actor.

"Theatre mainly, my darlings. But my old bones became a bit creaky to keep treading the boards. And I've always been a dabbler, haven't I Barry? Barry's the real artist among us." He revealed that Barry had been a theatre set designer, which was how they had met.

"I did think he owed you a rather more sincere apology than he gave you," Elizabeth said to Sera. The others agreed.

Sera said that she really didn't mind. "It was an educational experience. Now I know what it's like for the models. I could barely manage ten minutes, goodness knows how they sit still for hours."

"We thought you were quite charming, didn't we Barry? Very professional. Besides, most models move and take frequent breaks. Is this your first time in a life drawing class?"

Sera confessed that it was. "I study art at school but what I really want to do is portraiture. We don't get any opportunity to have actual models in art lessons so that's why I signed up here. I also thought the extra classes might help with my college application."

"After tonight, I should think you're owed a glowing reference," Jasper said. "Talented young artist, displays fine form in class." He lifted his wine glass in toast to Sera with a roguish wink, and she blushed.

She hoped she wouldn't lose her nerve when it came to attending next week's class. The reality of what she had done was only just beginning to sink in.

2. A shock at school

"You what?!"

Lois was half shocked, half laughing when Sera finally managed to tell her about the impromptu modelling session. It was the first day of the new school term and they were on their way to the art room.

"It was no big deal. Only for a few minutes," Sera said.

Her best friend couldn't stop laughing. "Only you, Sera, would deal with some rude idiot by taking your clothes off. For God's sake don't try that here."

Sera could hardly imaging doing so before Mr Billings, who taught art and history of art. He was a very conservative man who suffered agonies over works featuring scantily-clad nymphs or the Virgin nursing. From what they could work out he'd spent three years at art school painting nothing but bowls of fruit and vases of flowers.

"I can just about manage to keep my clothes on in front of Billy," Sera said.

"No one would be more relieved to hear that than him. So what was it like?"

"What was what like?"

Lois rolled her eyes. "Posing nude in front of people. Weren't you embarrassed? Weren't you cold?"

Sera actually had to think about it. Had she been cold? "No, there was a small electric heater there." Now she remembered that the teacher had switched it on and positioned it towards her just before she slipped the kimono off. He had been capable of some small consideration at least.

"And the nude thing?"

"Weirdly it was okay," Sera told her.

Lois tossed her curls. Their chestnut was currently streaked with strands of purple, blue and maroon. Lois's elder sister was a hair stylist so Lois often played guinea pig for her more experimental designs. "I hardly see how. You get embarrassed just wearing a swimming costume to the pool. I don't see how you managed to flash your fanny at a roomful of perfect strangers."

Put like that, nor did Sera. "It was weird. It wasn't like being naked normally: exposed in a vulnerable way, with people judging your body. It felt more like being a shop dummy or a statue. Anyway, they were all gay or women. Except for one bearded bloke, who looked like Mr Billings."

Thinking about it, there was only one man in the room who had seemed fully red-blooded and capable of that kind of attention.

The art teacher himself.

Sera remembered how the look in his eye had changed the moment he realised she wasn't a model. Suddenly he had seen her as human again, and female. She tried to explain this to Lois. "It's like the gender dynamic suddenly returned."

"You mean he eyed you up?" Lois asked.

Nothing quite that blatant. "It was more of an awareness. I probably read too much into it because I was so aware of him. Honestly Lo, if he hadn't been such a horrible, rude, angry idiot he would have been incredibly attractive."

Lois gave her a knowing grin. "You mean he was both, don't you? Admit it."

Sera hated to admit it but Lois was right. "Maybe."

"I wish I'd signed up for the course now. If he ever goes out to that pub with you, you'll have to invite me along," Lois said.

It didn't seem likely. He had appeared more like the kind of teacher who kept his distance and didn't become over friendly with his students.

* * *

Mr Billings wasn't there when they arrived, so she and Lois set themselves up in their preferred places. The aroma of art through the ages - or at least the couple of decades the art room had been in use - swirled around Sera. Oil paint, clay dust, charcoal and paper: she found it strangely intoxicating. It helped transport her to another world where she could forget about school and family and university applications and simply lose herself in lines and colours.

"Where's Old Billy Billings?" someone asked.

"No idea."

Sera was just fiddling with a piece of putty eraser in her pencil case when she heard the teacher arrive. Chairs scraped on the floor as people sat up and a murmur went around the room.

Sera looked up.

"What the hell are you doing here?"

It couldn't be. Her mouth fell open, she froze.

Tall, dark and furious, it was her art teacher nemesis from the other night. Once again he was glaring at her, his gaze hostile.

As quickly as he had lost his composure he regained it. "I'm Mr Marek. I'm replacing Mr Billings who as some of you may know has taken a sabbatical." No one knew this, faces around the room wore surprise and curiosity. "For today, so I can see your individual styles, you can sketch..." his eyes hurriedly looked around the room for an object, and fell on a hideously painted urn that a previous student had abandoned years before. He picked it up and slammed it down in the centre of the main table. "This. Pencil, charcoal, I don't care. And you," he pointed directly at Sera, "can see me outside."

Lois was boiling over with curiosity but Sera couldn't explain.

"You can't be in trouble already?" her friend Joel hissed as Sera, her face burning, made her way outside. She had no time to gather herself together before the irate Mr Marek stood before her.

He seemed to tower over her. He was well over six foot - over a head taller than her - so it wasn't surprising.

"So? I repeat, what the hell are you doing here?" His eyes were slate grey, unyielding.

This was at least easy to answer. though Sera pushed back a strand of hair nervously. "This is my art class, I'm a pupil at St Christopher's," she told him.

Mr Marek was silent for several moments. "How old are you?"

"Seventeen." Just like pretty much everyone at the start of September in their final year of school.

He swore. "Underage? And you thought you would compromise my class like that?"

"You asked me to. Demanded, in fact." Sera's confidence was returning as she now grew angry as well.

"Clearly you should have had the common sense not to comply, given your age, if nothing else."

None of the others had said anything. "It's not illegal. Look at Page Three." The British tabloid newspapers regularly featured topless models like Samantha Fox who were as young as sixteen.

The art teacher winced. "Life drawing is hardly glamour modelling. Regardless, I don't deal with minors."

Sera, still annoyed, felt emboldened. "It didn't seem to bother you the other night when you arranged me on your couch."

She met his gaze. There was a brief flicker in his eyes of something she couldn't define. Was he recalling the scene? She could smell the same faint scent of cologne or deodorant that he had worn the other night, and it brought it all back vividly into her mind.

To her surprise he gave a low laugh. "Trust me, if you think that was me arranging you on my couch, you have a great deal to learn."

Sera's stomach gave a strange flip at his tone.

He continued. "Seeing as I am apparently stuck with you as a pupil in both my workplaces, you will behave appropriately from now on. No messing around. Concentrate on your work. You will call me Mr Marek here and at the community centre, regardless of how the others address me. Now get inside and join the class."

He turned abruptly and went back into the room.

Sera was left beyond outrage. How dare he speak to her like that? She was one of the most conscientious students doing Art A-level, as so much of her future depended on the result. Yet he had already judged her to be some kind of troublemaker.

She knew Lois was going to be absolutely burning to know what was going on. Sera was also burning to vent, so they both spent the lesson looking at the clock and willing its hands to move faster.

3. Drawing instruction

The model this week was a portly middle aged man. If only he had been booked for the first class, Sera thought, there might never have been the mix up.

Mr Marek gave no indication of having had dealings with Sera elsewhere. St Christopher's was not mentioned. He was coolly professional once again although he seemed less angry this time.

He stood looking at her easel for some time. Sera could barely swallow. She knew she was making a dog's breakfast of the fat man. His thigh seemed to be twice the width of his head.

"You're new to this, aren't you?" His tone was wryly amused.

"It's my first life drawing class," she admitted.

"It might have been an idea to seek help before embarking on... this," Mr Marek said.

Sera wanted to sink through the floor.

"May I?" Without waiting for her to respond he reached for the pastel she was holding. It was his custom to guide students' hands rather than directly take the chalk or pencil himself.

But when his hand closed over Sera's she felt a jolt and the pastel jerked against the page, smudging the already messy and overworked line.

She glanced back at him, nervous. He was so close to her, the linen of his rolled up sleeve brushing her arm. His forearm was well-muscled, sprinkled with dark hair.

"Can you just show me? It might be easier if you just..." Sera tailed off.

Mr Marek raised his eyebrows but took the pastel. He was directly behind her and she was finding it hard to breathe. What on earth was wrong with her being around this man? He was going to think she was feeble minded if she couldn't keep a grip of herself.

"Like this." A few quick strokes and magically the portly model was appearing on the paper before them. "Each part of the limb is its own three-dimensional segment, jointed at the hip, knee and ankle. See? So now you can foreshorten the thigh while keeping the proportions of the femur."

He made it look so easy. Sera said so.

His lips twisted. "When you've been doing this for as long as I have, the basic structure comes without effort."

"Well, thank you anyway."

There was faint amusement in Mr Marek's eyes. "It's what I'm here for." He moved onto the next student and Sera felt the tension drain from her body as he left.

She was exhausted - the first week back at school had plunged them straight back into the syllabus, with a tonne of homework. By Thursday night Sera was more than ready for the weekend.

But there was exhilaration too. She already loved this class. Drawing a live subject always roused adrenalin in Sera, that feeling of trying to capture someone on paper in a limited time. She wasn't finding limbs as fascinating as faces but it was all great experience.

Once she had got the hang of it better she would try another medium. Barry sketched straight in oils, not even outlining in pencil first, and there was real mastery in his brushstrokes. Winifred, the elderly lady, had a very delicate touch with watercolours. Everyone else used charcoal or pastels, but Sera loved how the single sweep of a brush stroke could define the contours of a body.

Despite her efforts to concentrate, Sera found her eyes moving from the life model to the back and shoulders of Mr Marek. He was powerfully built and she imagined he would have perfect contours under his shirt. At least if his muscular arms were anything to go by.

Concentrate, she told herself sternly. She could hardly start fantasising about someone who was not only her teacher, but had also made it clear he despised her.

There was a five minute break where the model got to stretch out and visit the bathroom if needed. Students tended to use it as an opportunity to chat and comment on one another's work.

"I'd love to be able to paint like you," Sera told Barry. "You seem to get the lines perfect the first time."

"You'll get there," Barry said.

"He's too modest," Jasper interrupted. "It's gift that you have, Barry my boy. I could spend a hundred years in this class and still make my dreadful botch ups." He looked at Sera's drawing. "Now that's not bad at all. All the more so if this is your first class, as I overheard you mention."

Sera had to be honest. "It's barely my work, after all the help I needed."

She saw Mr Marek's head turn towards her, overhearing. "It wasn't quite that bad," he told her. "The shading was competent."

Was this a compliment? Given how hostile he had been, it was very disarming to receive even a glimmer of praise.

Before Sera could wonder about it any more the model returned to take his place, in a different pose for the second hour, and the class continued. Sera tried to apply what Mr Marek had taught her to her second drawing. She found his advice made a real improvement.

Even as she tried to concentrate on her work she was keenly aware of the tall, dark haired figure moving from place to place in the room. He showed a genuine interest in everyone's work and treated even the more amateur artists with the same respect as the most experienced students.

* * *

"Once more unto the Norfolk Arms, dear friends," Jasper announced as the class were packing up their equipment. "You'll join us, of course?" he asked the art teacher.

"By all means."

Sera was surprised that Mr Marek had accepted. Perhaps something about Jasper's gallantry made the invitation hard to refuse.

She expected to have to make her own excuses and catch the bus but Jasper managed to coerce her into accepting as well. It was his tone, she thought. It was compelling, if not compelling enough to sway Bob or Winifred who claimed to prefer an early night.

As before, Sera, Elizabeth, Jasper and Barry entered the pub and went to the same table. "You go on ahead, I have to close up," Mr Marek had told them. Jasper had ascertained his choice of drink - a half of lager - so it would be there as soon as he arrived.

The pub was quiet again this week. A guy in a leather jacket was putting coins in the fruit machine and clearly losing. Two large men with moustaches sat on the same bar stools they had done last week, obviously regulars. Sera made a mental note never to add the place to the list, the next time she and Lois went on a bar crawl. It did not look like promising pulling territory.

"A very productive session tonight, don't you think?" Jasper asked everyone while they waited for Mr Marek to arrive.

"I'm afraid I got the shoulders all wrong," Elizabeth said. "After that it was all downhill." Sera had learnt that she was a horticulturalist by profession and had studied botanical drawing for many years. The life drawing class was a change in direction for her.

"Some weeks it works, some it doesn't," said Barry. He was a man of few words compared to Jasper. Yet when he did speak his words had a simplicity and substance to them.

Sera found herself biting a nail and then wondering why she was nervous. She knew the reason when her stomach jolted once Mr Marek entered the room.

He nodded to Jasper and thanked him for the beer. Then he turned to Sera. "Should you be in here?" His tone wasn't rude but it was cool.

Since Sera knew she shouldn't be in there, she didn't respond. She chewed her lip.

"Sera is seventeen, and these are licensed premises," Mr Marek told the others who were observing the interaction.

"Are you indeed? I would have put you at at least twenty-one," Jasper said. "Back in my long ago, highly disreputable boyhood I was patronising our local pub from the age of twelve. The landlord had a soft spot for me, of course. I dare say it did me no harm." He launched into a somewhat salacious anecdote about his uncle, a barmaid and his uncle's irate wife.

Sera realised that Jasper was deliberately steering the conversation away from her to gloss over the issue with her age and felt grateful to him. She was only a couple of months from turning eighteen, after all. She and Lois had been nightclubbing on fake ID for years anyway.

Mr Marek said nothing more and she could tell he was trying to ignore her. But a few times his gaze flicked to her, immediately moving away again if she met his eyes.

"You're not from the area originally?" Elizabeth asked him.

"No, my parents retired here a few years ago."

"And are they enjoying it?" Elizabeth, like Sera, had lived in the area her whole life.

"They were. My mother died four years ago." Mr Marek said this in a neutral tone but a shutter fell behind his eyes, at least from what Sera could see.

Sensing his discomfort, Elizabeth murmured a polite condolence and the conversation moved on.

The art teacher only stayed for one drink then made his excuses and left. Things felt flat after he had gone, though Jasper tried to nudge conversation.

"He's an artist, you know. Exhibited. Barry recognised his name."

"What is his name?" Sera was secretly glad to hear Elizabeth ask this since she didn't like to herself.

"Tarquin Marek. Rather splendid, isn't it? English mother, Hungarian father. Exhibited at the Royal Academy no less." Barry nodded in agreement, nursing his cider. "The real mystery is what he's doing in our quiet little backwater, rather than continuing his stellar trajectory in the art world."

Tarquin Marek. Tarquin the Proud was the last King of Rome, Sera remembered. It seemed a suitable name for the art teacher. Artistic and arrogant.

Everyone else left soon afterwards. Sera headed for the bus stop. It was dark but she enjoyed travelling home at night. It was peaceful. The bus stop was well lit and the short walk to her house was along a quiet suburban street. It gave her time to clear her head before having to face the stress and bustle of her family.

* * *

"You're late back."

The comment was made by Sera's stepmother, Marisa. Her tone wasn't accusatory as she had long ago given up on trying to argue with Sera about her whereabouts.

Still wearing her immaculate business suit, Marisa was heating up a pan on the stove. She was literally superwoman, Sera thought. She kept the house flawless and raised Sera's twin half-brothers as well as maintaining a high profile career in accountancy.

There was little love lost between the two of them. Years of failing to understand one another had done their damage. Marisa still couldn't understand why Sera didn't want to study business or finance, but rather "throw it all away" doing a degree in Fine Art.

Sera, who thought that doing finance would be throwing it all away, had never managed to convince her stepmother otherwise. These days they were civil to one another but simply very different people. Some days Sera regretted it, most days she didn't care.

They both adored the twins at least, which gave them some common ground.

"The people from the evening class all go down to the pub afterwards. The Norfolk Arms," Sera said. She wondered how Marisa would have reacted if she had found out about Sera's brief modelling experience in the first session.

"The Norfolk Arms?" Her father came into the kitchen, carrying a bottle of wine which he put in the fridge. "A bit of a rough spot, isn't it?"

"It was half empty," Sera told him.

"So what are your fellow students like?" her father asked. His own mother had been an illustrator so he was sympathetic to Sera's ambitions. But he ran a construction company himself and was a businessman at heart, so also understood Marisa's view. He generally tried to stay neutral between his wife and daughter, privately regretting that they had little affinity.

"There's only six of us. A bearded bloke, a nice old lady, another woman about your age," Sera said, indicating Marisa. She was aware that Elizabeth was a good ten years older than Marisa but wasn't sure how else to describe it. "Middle aged woman" sounded impolite. "Then an elderly gay couple from the theatre. They're fun."

"And the teacher is helpful?"

"He's okay." Sera wasn't sure if she should mention that he had turned out to be the new art teacher at St Christopher's as well. She decided not to say anything. She still wasn't sure how she felt about it all.

"As long as it doesn't distract you from the rest of your subjects," Marisa said. "Your other A-levels are just as important. You need something to fall back on if a career in art doesn't work out."

Sera mentally rolled her eyes as she set out cutlery and filled a jug with water for the table. "It's only a couple of hours per week. If I get swamped with assignments I can always skip a class." She had zero intention of skipping a class, but Marisa didn't need to know that.

Marisa looked appeased. "We do want you to do well." There was genuine concern on her face.

While her stepmother didn't know the real reason, it was true Sera was facing a major distraction that term. The very man teaching her art.

Mr Marek had got under her skin, that was for sure. That night as she lay in bed she couldn't stop thinking of him glaring at her, remembering his masculine aroma as he stood so close to her in class, and how his hand had felt touching her skin on the couch.

4. The sketch

"He's a murderer," Lois said. "Mr Marek ending up with both those jobs is more than a coincidence. He's clearly done away with Mr Billings and Miss Featherdale for his own career gain."

"Fotheringay."

"Whatever. You need to start investigating the Strange Disappearance of Ethel Fotheringay." Lois made it sound like the title of a detective novel.

Sera vaguely remembered someone mentioning that the missing art teacher's name was Elsie but didn't bother to correct Lois. "I can think of any number of reasons why he might have ended up with more than one art teaching job. Going down to the job centre and applying for all art teaching jobs for starters."

They were sitting at a table under a tree. It was lunchtime and the weather was fortunately mellow that day. Deep gold autumn sunlight and a clear, icy blue sky. Sera imagined the colours that would be used to paint it, mentally mixing up a palette.

Joel was sketching a coat onto the paper bag his sandwich had been in. "I hardly think teaching us lot would be described as career gain. I wonder why he's really here. He's an actual artist, isn't he?"

"Apparently so." Sera wondered how Joel knew. She hadn't mentioned Jasper's revelation to them, not wanting to give them the idea that she was overly interested in their art teacher. Because she found herself frequently wondering about him despite a determined attempt to keep him out of her head.

"I heard one of the other staff mentioning it. Also you needn't worry about Billy because he is actually on sabbatical. He's doing something in Florence," Joel said.

"Unless it's a massive conspiracy and they're all in on it," Lois said. "Seriously though, what kind of an artist is Sera's Mr Marek?"

"He's not my Mr Marek!" Sera protested.

Lois twisted a magenta strand of hair that she had isolated from the other colours. "He glares at you. I suspect that means he's interested. After all he's seen you in the buff, hasn't he? He probably keeps thinking about it. It must be a bit kinky, him now seeing you in your school uniform."

"He glares at me because he hates me," Sera said. "He also thinks I'm useless. He had to practically redraw my last sketch from scratch."

Joel, dissatisfied with his design, crumpled it up. "I can't comment on him seeing you in the buff, as I haven't personally had that privilege, but he's glaring at you because you're getting to him. Us men are simple creatures. If he merely hated you, he'd find it very easy to ignore you."

Sera picked up the crumpled paper bag and unfolded it. She smoothed it out and gave the design a critical eye. "This is good, you shouldn't just throw it away. I'd wear it."

"In that case it's a total failure then since it was supposed to be a man's coat," Joel told her.

"Let me have a look." Lois grabbed it. "It looks unisex to me. Anyway, back to our new art teacher, I wonder what kind of artist he is? Is he famous?"

Joel shrugged. "I'll see if I can find out."

Sera silently hoped he would find out more information about Mr Marek. She was more curious than she wanted to admit about him. "His first name's Tarquin. His father's Hungarian and he - Mr Marek, that is - has exhibited at the Royal Academy."

Lois shot Joel a smug grin at this. "You have been doing your homework," she said to Sera.

"Not me, one of the other people from the evening class found it out. They think there's a bit of a mystery about him," Sera told her.

"If there is, we'll have to solve it. Come on, we're going to be late for class."

Sera was working on a sketch of Joel while they waited for Mr Marek to arrive for their next lesson. She had drawn both Joel and Lois a dozen or more times before. So she knew the shape of Joel's eye and the twist of his lips almost by heart.

Lois looked over. "You are getting good," she said. "And fast."

Speed was one of Sera's goals given her future plans so she was happy to hear this.

"People might even pay for them, if you made them flattering enough," Lois said.

This was also one of Sera's distant, dearest hopes. "What would you pay for it?" she asked Lois.

"I wouldn't pay anything for it because you're my mate and I'd get it for free. But if I wasn't, I don't know, maybe five quid? Ten quid, even."

It wasn't exactly Sotheby's price level but it was a start. Given that Sera could sketch a reasonable likeness in about five minutes, and have a more complete picture done in ten, if people lined up back-to-back that would be sixty pounds an hour. She started to fantasise about actually doing this, and wondering where she would find clients when a shadow fell over her.

Her pencil froze as the paper was slipped away and held up by Mr Marek, who scrutinised it.

"Did you do this?"

"It's all mine," Sera told him.

For several seconds he gazed at the paper, his expression unreadable.

His next question took her by surprise. "Why do you leave the faces blank in evening class?"

Sera was disconcerted. "I wanted to do a portraiture class, but..."

"So why choose life drawing?"

Why would he never let her finish? "Because there wasn't one. I thought life drawing would be the next best thing, and so..."

Mr Marek raised his eyebrows. "So I'm only second best?"

Sera felt her face flame and stared down at the table to hide it. "No. I'm finding the class really productive. I just thought I should concentrate on the figure because I haven't done that before." She moved her eyes back up to meet his and saw a mocking glint in them. He was amused, not angry.

"If you want to paint portraits, by all means focus on that. I think learning to draw the entire human form would be useful to you as an artist, but you should do what you need to do." He put the sketch back down, and as he left - before Sera could react - he said: "You have considerable talent." His eyes lingered on her for a moment before he left.

Sera was stunned and strangely shaky. As she started to get her other pencils ready for the morning's exercise, her fingers were shaking. She could tell that Lois and Joel were giving her curious glances but she needed time to process this.

He had said she was talented. *He had called her an artist.*

Given she had assumed he hated her, this seemed like rare praise.

"Well, well," Joel muttered and Sera kicked him.

"There's no well well."

"Well, well, well."

Lois was giggling. "You're the colour of a beetroot. Anyone would think you had a crush on him."

Sera was mortified. "No way. I was just surprised that he didn't shout at me."

"I'd say he wants to do more than shout at you, the way he looks at you."

It was highly unlikely, as much as Sera would have liked it to be true. They all got on with that day's exercise.

Sera noticed that Mr Marek spent a lot of time helping Janette, a girl on the other table, who wore hearing aids and also had very thick glasses. Despite this she was quite talented at art, particularly abstract works with lots of bold colour. Mr Billings had tended to ignore her as he liked figurative art and Janette struggled with fine details. Sera was glad to see her finally getting some teaching attention.

"So are we going clubbing this weekend?" Lois whispered.

"Definitely." Hitting the town and getting wasted would be a good way to keep Sera's mind off things.

"What about you, Joel?"

Joel pretended to shudder. "A night of watching you two dance around your handbags? I don't think so. They've got a guest DJ at Orion, so I'm going there." Orion was unofficially the only gay club in town.

"We don't carry handbags as you well know, and you ought to talk about embarrassing dancing. One drink and you're the shame of the town." Lois quickly buttoned her lip as she saw the art teacher glaring at them. At least I'm not the only one incurring his wrath, Sera thought.

5. Dangerous dance

"This was the worst decision ever."

Lois, a drink in her hand, was trying to get up a staircase against a never-ending flow of drunken people. Aether, the town's main nightclub, was nearly bursting at the seams. There was no air conditioning and it was a hot, sweaty crush of bodies. The problem was that they weren't really the kind of bodies that Sera or Lois were into. There didn't seem to be a hot guy in sight.

"I also feel like someone's grandmother," Sera said.

This was the problem with clubs that turned a blind eye to fake ID. Sera and Lois had been clubbing since they were fourteen. Now they were nearly legal drinking age, everyone else in the club was years younger. Mainly girls, since it was easier to fake being eighteen if you could slap on make-up and high heels.

So now Sera and Lois felt among the oldest females there.

"It's like a youth club isn't it? Let's go somewhere else."

Getting out was easier said than done due to the crowds. Sera dreaded to think how they would evacuate the place if there was ever a fire. Aether was built in the hollowed out structure of what was formerly a large town house. There were several storeys with dance floors and bars connected by various staircases that wound around.

Plus a basement which was so hot and dark that Sera crunched and swallowed ice cubes whenever they danced there to try and cool down. The bartenders didn't charge for a glass of ice so it was cheaper than buying a drink.

"Where shall we go then?" Sera asked as they finally got outside and felt the chill night air bite their skin.

"I don't know, what's open late? It's nearly closing time for most places. The Retro is open until 1am, isn't it?" It was the other side of town but worth the walk if it was the only place open. It was also near Orion, so if they felt like it they could gatecrash Joel's night out.

Sera had never been sure about The Retro. As bars went it always seemed a little bit dark and a little bit cliquey. It was an odd mix of style and grunge, half bar, half club. The crowd there was also quite a bit older, they'd definitely be among the youngest people in the place if they managed to get in.

Which they did. It wasn't hard to get admitted being young, female and in a super short skirt when the average bouncer was a straight male, more interested in getting hot females through the door while keeping out drunken, aggressive males. At this time of night people were starting to spill out of regular bars, many of them the worse for wear. The doormen had their work cut out.

Lois got them two gin and tonics because the drinks fluoresced in the black light downstairs, which always looked eye catching. There was a small dance floor but people tended to sway and jiggle a bit rather than actually dance. Nearly everyone was wearing black.

"Pretty much all these people are just sad office workers by day, much as they may like to think they look like The Cure," Lois said after some woman gave her a nasty glare and muttered something that sounded like "tarts". Having come from a nightclub they were both wearing skimpy, tight mini-dresses and getting more male attention than women dressing down in jeans.

One group of men clearly weren't office workers though. When Sera and Lois got onto the dancefloor they were soon surrounded by half a dozen large guys who turned out be some visiting rugby team. This was more like it! Typical, of course, that they were only visitors and not full-time residents of the town.

If you liked big burly men you were spoilt for choice. Lois was soon hanging off the neck of one of them but Sera found herself holding back. Something just didn't click for her that night.

As her friend was quite happy on the dance floor Sera slipped to the bathroom. She was looking fine: her make-up intact, her hair was okay. Through the narrow window in the bathroom she could see the moon above the buildings outside. A thin, bright silver crescent, only a couple of days past the new moon.

She shivered, without knowing why.

Then she stepped outside and her blood ran really cold.

There, just by the adjacent wall and glaring right at her, was Mr Marek.

* * *

You could get into a huge trouble if a teacher caught you out on the town underage. Sera froze, then frantically wondered what to do.

Walk by him and ignore him? Give him a brief nod and hope he turned a blind eye?

Fall at his feet prostrate and beg him not to report them?

Yeah, like that was ever going to happen. She chose the ignore option, perhaps she could pretend she hadn't even seen him and he would do the same.

"Sera."

No luck with that then. She winced, prayed, and turned to him. "Mr Marek?"

"Underage and in a licensed premises yet again?" He stood there looking tall and severe, and incredibly good looking.

There wasn't a lot she could say in response. "I bet you didn't wait until you were eighteen to start drinking."

"Probably not. That doesn't make it right for you to be here. Let alone dressed like that." His eyes ran up and down her dress, which was admittedly very short, and his gaze made her burn inside.

Sera felt daring. "Given how much more of me you've seen, I can't see why this should bother you." On "this" she ran her hand over the top of her dress, drawing his attention to the neckline and the swell of her breasts.

His face betrayed no reaction. "That was perfectly professional."

"Was it?" Sera remembered how the way he looked at her had changed once the other model had arrived.

"Until I realised you weren't a professional model, yes."

Was this an admission? She looked up into his eyes - he was so much taller than her - and was certain she saw the same

30

attraction there that she felt. Why did he have to be her teacher? If only he was one of the guys playing rugby she could easily have pulled him onto the dance floor, probably have given him her phone number at the end of the night.

Sera decided to be daring. "Are you going to dance?" There were actually people dancing at this point, as a recent club hit was playing.

"Not to this."

"It's not your type of music?" she asked.

"Not exactly."

"Do you ever dance?"

He looked straight at her. "Not with my students."

Something in Sera gave an absurd little thrill at his use of "my". It wasn't intended to be possessive - after all he could equally have applied the same term to Barry or Jasper - but she liked the sense of association with him.

"I guess I'll have to go and dance with that lot then." She indicated the rugby players who were all over Lois.

Sera hadn't meant her words to rile Mr Marek, she genuinely intended to simply go and dance with the rugby team. But his eyes darkened when he saw the players jostling around Lois and a muscle clenched in his jaw.

"I'll dance with you."

His tone was one of command, not acceptance of her invitation. Too shocked to react, Sera walked to the mass of moving bodies and Mr Marek followed her.

They faced one another and feeling strangely giddy, Sera began moving to the music in front of him. Out of the corner of her eye she could see Lois's mouth drop open. Sera knew her friend would drag her off the dance floor and to the cloakroom, wanting to know exactly what was happening. So she deliberately avoided looking in her direction.

Instead she cast her eyes up towards Mr Marek's face. He towered over her and everyone else, he was at least as tall and well-built as any of the rugby players. Yet despite his height and strength he had a masculine grace as he moved that made the rugby guys look clumsy.

They weren't really dancing together, just swaying in front of each other. Mr Marek was so incredibly attractive. Sera was close enough to sense the heat of his body and the trace of his aftershave. His eyes glinted as the lights flashed past them, his hair as black as midnight. His lips were firm and perfectly sculpted but unsmiling. Sera felt a magnetic force drawing her towards him.

What would it be like to kiss him? To have him crush her against him, with all the anger she could perceive in him flooding out into a violent embrace?

Desire gave Sera a rush of confidence. She moved closer to him, took his hands and put them on her hips. He dropped them instantly but she smiled at him, a sexy smile hyped up by alcohol and adrenalin, and tried again.

This time he let them linger there. He was looking at her, transfixed, his expression hard but failing to mask a flicker of attraction. More than a flicker.

Sera closed her eyes. She swayed closer to the music and to Mr Marek. I can't believe I'm dancing with him, she thought. His hands only touched her lightly but her body burned and tingled under their impression.

She wanted to put her arms around his neck, draw up to him and feel his lips on hers, but she sensed it would be a step too far. Instead she used her hands to scoop up her own hair, twisting it on top of her head. Raising her arms meant her breasts were lifted towards him. He took a step back, breaking contact with her, and swore under his breath.

Sera smiled again and tried to return his hands to her hips but instead he gripped her arms and pressed them down against her sides, preventing her from reaching out to touch him.

The song finished soon afterwards and Mr Marek released Sera's arms and left the dance floor.

"This never happened," he told her, his face unsmiling.

Sera watched him leave, going upstairs and she guessed out into the night. Everything felt flat and dull once he had gone, though certain parts of her were still burning with nerves and excitement from the memory of his touch. As anticipated, Lois soon dragged her off to the bathroom.

"What the hell? You dancing with Mr Marek. How did that happen?"

"I asked him," Sera admitted. "He was very reluctant."

"He looked more like he wanted to eat you. Or kill you," Lois added.

Sera wouldn't have minded either. "He smells amazing."

"He's your teacher, he's supposed to smell of art books and oil paint."

Oil paint... just the thought of that aroma seemed erotic to Sera right then, because it made her think of Mr Marek.

"The look on your face," Lois said. "You're in a dream world. Please don't tell me you've gone and got a crush on him. I know what Joel and I said, but we were only joking."

Sera felt dejected. "You mean about him glaring at me?"

"All that, yes. It's true he does glare at you - glower might be a better term for it - but I'm sure Joel's just winding us up about it having any significance."

Now Sera wasn't sure if she should feel disappointed or heartened by Lois's words.

"He'll probably completely ignore me next class," she said.

Lois made a face at herself in the mirror and pouted, having reapplied her lipstick.

"I guess it could be worse."

"How could it?" Sera asked.

"You could have taken all your clothes off and given him a striptease. Oh wait - that's right - you already did." With a wicked grin Lois slipped back out into the bar before Sera could react.

Monday was certainly going to be interesting. Sera felt a thrill of fear and anticipation just thinking about it.

6. In the rain

As anticipated, Mr Marek completely ignored Sera the next week in school. This was easy enough to do without people noticing as the class was large enough that he could simply concentrate on other students. He still gave brief critique and guidance for her work, but the absolute minimum.

Watching him spend much more time with others, and being more relaxed and friendly with them, was really hard. Mr Marek wasn't exactly the sort of light-hearted teacher who joked around, so on the rare occasions he smiled it was devastating. But he never smiled around her.

Sera was crushed even though she had expected this. She found it almost impossible to stop trying to sneak a glance at him in class and catch his eye, but she tried to discipline herself. She didn't want Mr Marek to realise she cared.

Lois and Joel saw how things were and tried to buoy her spirits. Lois had of course told Joel all about the nightclub.

"It's very pointed, his ignoring you," Joel said. "That means he's not actually indifferent, he's just trying to be."

They were currently supposed to be blending pastels to represent shadows in different coloured lights. Sera was finding it hard to concentrate on the fruit bowl in front of them. She found herself thinking about how the light hit the art teacher's skin: the shadows under his cheekbones, the changing grey of his eyes.

"Or he's trying to send me a message that he truly doesn't want anything more to do to me," Sera said.

"I doubt it. He wouldn't have danced with you otherwise, he looked like he wanted to devour you. Like he was wrestling with himself. After all, if word got out that he was fraternising and dancing with students in a club, he'd be in serious trouble," Lois pointed out.

Somehow Sera wasn't sure that Mr Marek would really care about getting fired. Presumably he did need the teaching position or he wouldn't have taken it. But she suspected he was the kind of person to simply walk out rather than beg and plead to keep a job.

"God this is dull," Joel said. He loathed still life. "It was bad enough having fruit and flowers every week with old Billings."

Lois picked up a fuchsia coloured pastel and started colouring in an implausibly pink hue on the side of the banana she had drawn. Unlike the other two she had no ambitions in anything art related as a career. She had only chosen art because the other two were doing it, and it seemed like less effort than Chemistry or History.

"Fruit and flowers is what they say in the record industry to mean hookers and cocaine," she said.

Joel was curious. "Which is which?"

"No idea. My sister mentioned it. Someone she trained with did the styling for a music video."

"Anyone famous?" Joel asked.

"Not that I'd heard of. I suppose they might be eventually," Lois said.

"You should get a signed photo then."

Joel fell silent as Mr Marek's gaze swept over them. "I trust you're managing to get some work done amid all the conversation?"

No one dared speak after this. Instead they concentrated furiously on the shading, Lois decided to turn half of the pineapple blue. When the art teacher's back was turned, she whispered to Sera: "I wonder if he commands his partners to be quiet in bed while he gets his work done?"

Sera felt her face flame at the thought of it and had to swallow a giggle. She briefly glanced at Mr Marek only to find him looking at her. She hadn't felt self-conscious in front of him in the bar, and previous lessons had been fine. But something in his expression reminded her what he had seen of her.

Was he remembering it too? For a second she felt completely exposed, as though he could see beneath her clothes. She bit her lip, trying to regain her composure.

Mr Marek held her gaze for a moment, then moved on. The spell was broken but Sera was sure she had felt a connection.

* * *

In Thursday's evening class Mr Marek was coolly professional towards Sera, but civil enough that his coolness didn't attract attention or remark. It was harder to hide these tensions in such a small class.

They were sketching a female model this time. Sera noticed how professional the art teacher was: he ensured the models were comfortable, adjusted the electric heater, and kept a careful eye on the clock so they could take their scheduled breaks.

She wondered if he would ever join them in sketching so they could get an idea of his style and proficiency, but she didn't dare to ask him.

"That's beautiful, quite arrestingly lovely," Jasper commented on Sera's half-completed work as they all stopped for a rest and recharge. "Don't you think so, Elizabeth?" he said, as Elizabeth stood next to him.

"It's wonderful, you're very talented," Elizabeth told Sera, who felt embarrassed but pleased. She had not done too much with the figure this time, deciding to focus instead on the head and shoulders.

The model was quite an ordinary looking woman, around fifty, of average build with a bob of dark hair. Yet Sera had picked out a charm in her face and an intelligence in her eyes that the others - focused as they were on the entirety of her body - hadn't included.

"If you draw like that, I imagine you could be very successful," Jasper said. "It's not even that you've flattered her, for it's all there. You've simply picked out all the right notes. It makes me view her in quite a different light."

Barry came over and was frowning as he gazed at Sera's sketch. "I'd say that was not bad at all."

Given Barry's own huge talent this felt like great praise. It put pressure on Sera not to mess the drawing up by overworking it in the second half.

When they resumed, Sera felt Mr Marek come and stand behind her. For a while he said nothing and she tried to ignore him while she added some chalk highlights to the model's collarbone.

"It's complete as it is. You can stop. Start again," he told her.

"Start again?"

"Try a second sketch, from another angle if you like."

Sera wanted to ask him more about what he thought of her drawing. "Complete" didn't really convey whether he liked it or not. To her chagrin she found that she desperately sought his approval. Just one positive word from him would have eclipsed all of Jasper's praise.

For the second hour she decided to do a regular life drawing of the whole body rather than a portrait. What she was learning was definitely helping with her portraiture. She had a much better understanding of the neck and shoulders as a structure and the angle of the head. It was weirdly analytical to think of the human form this way but it gave her portraits far better perspective.

Sera wasn't able to join the others that night in the pub as she had a massive essay to get done by the next day. She also suspected that Mr Marek wouldn't go, to avoid her. And if she was being really honest with herself, the main reason she wanted to go was in case he also went.

Outside it was dark with the sickly amber light of a street light shining down by the bus stop, when it suddenly started to rain quite heavily. There had been dampness in the air before and some drizzle, but Sera hadn't anticipated this. In fairness, she didn't tend to check the weather forecasts.

But there she stood, getting increasingly cold and soaked, having missed the last bus by five minutes and having to wait twenty more for the next one.

A car drew up alongside and the window wound down. It was Mr Marek who had just driven out of the community centre car park and around the corner. He obviously hadn't gone to the Norfolk Arms either.

"What are you doing?"

Sera thought that was obvious. "I'm waiting for the bus."

"I meant why are you standing there in the pouring rain with no raincoat or umbrella?"

Before Sera could answer, he spoke again. "Get in, I'll give you a lift."

"It's only a few minutes away," she told him. This wasn't true but he didn't know that.

"For God's sake, Sera, just get in the car and I'll drive you home."

Once again she found herself powerless to resist his instruction. Slipping into the front passenger seat, she was tempted to make a joke about getting into cars with strange men, but seeing the grim set of his jaw she thought it wiser to remain silent.

"So?"

Sera was confused. She repeated it to him. "So...?"

"So where do you live? Or do you just want me to drive around in circles all night?"

Actually she did. Just being with her art teacher was a thrill, even if he clearly couldn't stand her. Still, at least he didn't hate her enough to let her drown in the rain.

Sera gave him directions, privately fretting in case he thought it was too far. "You could just drop me on the corner. I have to walk back from there when I get the bus anyway."

Mr Marek turned to glance at her. "That would save all of thirty seconds. It's hardly far in the first place."

He should be relieved then, Sera thought, not to have to spend any longer with her than his chivalry had demanded. "Thank you."

He said nothing but continued to drive. Sera tried to concentrate on the road ahead, giving him directions when required, but couldn't resist flicking her eyes to his profile.

He was so devastatingly handsome. His features were literally perfect: strong, well sculpted, utterly masculine. Sera longed to paint him. She wished she had Barry's skill: she could visualise how his oils would perfectly capture the angles of Mr Marek's face and the set of his jaw.

All too soon they reached her street. Despite being dark and shadowy from all the trees at this time of night, it was a good neighbourhood and relatively safe to walk alone in, even at night.

While Sera undid her seatbelt and gathered her art things together, Mr Marek got out of his side and opened the door for her. She was astonished at the courtesy, given it was still raining, and stammered her thanks.

"My pleasure," he told her, in a way that made it sound anything but.

Before she turned from him to go up her driveway his eyes raked over her, down her body and back up to her face. He must be thinking how much like a drowned rat she looked, as her hair had been soaked from just the couple of minutes she had stood in the rain. Sera felt self-conscious and at a disadvantage. She briefly wished she was wearing one of Marisa's power suits and heels so she would feel more assertive.

"Goodbye, and thank you," she told him.

Mr Marek said nothing, not even "see you in class", so Sera left him for the warmth and dry of her home.

7. A proposition

On Saturday morning Sera had the blissful peace of the house to herself. Much as she loved her brothers they were two nightmarish balls of noise and energy when she wanted to relax. They had gone with her father and Marisa to visit Marisa's parents for the weekend, and would stay there overnight.

Sera was always welcome to visit Marisa's parents, they treated her as though she was their own grandchild, but she wanted some time to herself and they understood that she had a lot of assignments in this final year of school.

Turning on the kettle and putting a slice of bread into the toaster, Sera considered calling Lois and hanging out later that day. They could go into town in the afternoon and go shopping and decide what to do that night: clubbing or staying in to watch movies. Assuming Lois didn't have a date, which Sera was pretty sure she didn't.

Sera rarely threw parties when her parents were away because the prospect of returning the house to Marisa's exacting standards filled her with dread. It was so easy for a house to get completely trashed as well.

But having Lois over was fine. Even Lois and Joel, though he sometimes got bored when they talked girl stuff.

Sera looked outside of the window. It was grey and raining but the sky had a brightness that suggested it might clear up later. She hoped so. Going shopping in the rain was never fun, as most of the shops they liked to visit were in the High Street rather than a mall.

Still wearing her dressing gown, she was about to jump in the shower when the phone rang. It was Lois.

"Hello, you must be psychic. I was going to call you right after I shower. Want to do something this afternoon, go shopping, maybe?"

"Sure," Lois said. "I was actually ringing about tonight. My sister is going to some party and we're invited. Some people in a huge house the other side of town. We don't even need to bring booze, apparently there'll be loads there."

It sounded good to Sera. Better than paying the entrance fee to Aether and being surrounded by fifteen-year-olds.

"There should be loads of hot guys," Lois said. "The guy whose house it is does Phys Ed so all these sporty university students should be coming."

Normally this would have been a big enticement to Sera but she found it hard to work up much enthusiasm. She didn't want to admit to herself why, though her mind kept wandering to The Retro and wondering if they went there, whether they might again bump into...

The doorbell rang, shrilly.

"I've got to go, there's someone at the door. Meet you by the fountain at midday?"

"Sounds great, see you there," Lois said and they ended the call.

Sera went to the door, expecting a neighbour or a Jehovah's Witness. They'd just have to cope with seeing her in her nightwear. Her robe, although made of rather slinky satin, at least covered what it needed to.

"Hello?"

She stopped, shocked.

It was Mr Marek. What was he doing here?

He looked gorgeous but wrecked. His hair was tousled and he had shadows under his eyes. He also hadn't shaved that morning, which made his face look darker and more angled.

"Sera."

His gaze dropped, instantly noticing what she was wearing. His eyes burned through the silken fabric of her night slip where it showed at the front of her robe. She realised how low cut it was and felt paralysed with embarrassment. If only she had quickly thrown on some jeans.

She couldn't try and cover herself up because it would make it even more obvious.

Sera had absolutely no idea why her art teacher was standing at her door. He seemed as lost for words as she was. To bluntly ask "why are you here?" seemed rude. To say "can I help?" sounded presumptuous. But he was just standing there, staring at her.

Seconds ticked by. Sera was starting to worry that the neighbours would notice her standing at the door, in a state of near undress, with a male visitor. Enough curtain-twitching and gossiping went on as it was.

Eventually he spoke. "Are your parents in?"

"They're away for the weekend."

Something momentarily flared in his eyes then was extinguished. "I won't come in."

Sera stood there, awkwardly. She panicked that she must look a sight with no make-up, her hair messy from bed. She tried to smooth back a lock of hair behind her ear.

This really was the last way on earth she would ever plan to greet her art teacher.

Before she could ask Mr Marek what he wanted he spoke again, and what he said took her breath away.

"I need to paint you. I need you to pose for me. I can't get the image of you in class out of my head, and until I have it down on canvas I can't concentrate on any other work."

* * *

Sera was shocked. Whatever she might have expected Mr Marek to say, it would never have been this.

Pose for him? Did he mean.... nude?

She supposed the prospect shouldn't freak her out. After all, it wasn't as though she hadn't done that before.

Struggling to come up with a response, she simply asked: "when?"

Relief softened his frown.

"You'll do it? I'll pay you a professional fee."

Sera hadn't actually meant to agree to pose for him, she had simply wanted to ask more questions to play for time. She wanted to ask "why me?" Surely if he wanted to paint a life model he could have asked any of the actual professionals hired at his classes?

But she was intrigued.

"How long would it take?" She imagined maybe a couple of hours, like the classes.

"I can't say. Several weeks, depending on how often you're available for sessions," Mr Marek told her.

Several weeks? The surprise was clear on her face.

"It's not merely for a sketch, Sera. I want to do a full canvas."

Sera had so many questions. Where would she pose? Why did he want to do this? How would it all happen? What would people say?

Before she could start to ask him, he continued. "We'll need to be discreet about this. I recognise there are ethical issues, but it's for art, not anything inappropriate."

"So you mean life modelling, like for the class?" Sera couldn't bring herself to say "nude" or "naked".

"Just as you were. That exact position, in fact. I'll fix it up the same."

She took a deep breath in and out. The world seemed at once to be moving very slowly and also rushing around her. He was the stillness at the centre.

"I guess... okay then. I'll try." She wasn't sure that she could pose successfully for him: just the few minutes she had tried in the art class had ended up being horribly uncomfortable. "But only on one condition."

Mr Marek frowned, concerned about what she might be about to demand.

"Central heating or a really warm heater."

His face relaxed again and she was rewarded with one of his rare smiles. "Certainly."

"When did you want to start?" She hoped not today. She needed to get her thoughts together. As well as get to some waxing and trimming.

"I thought next Saturday, if that works for you."

It was a whole week away and she usually spent Saturdays with her friends. "What time?"

"Midday? Until around two o'clock? The days being so short is limiting in terms of light. At my place, I'll give you the address."

High noon. It sounded perfect. She'd still have the rest of the afternoon and the whole evening and night free. She and Lois never hit the town before nine anyway, it was dead before that hour. Whether she would feel like the usual pub crawl after two hours of lying naked in front of her sexy but hostile, remote but demanding art teacher remained to be seen.

"Twelve to two works for me," Sera said.

"Thank you."

At that moment she sensed how relieved yet also conflicted he was. There was still doubt in his eyes though she wasn't sure why. Maybe he already regretted asking her, taking the risk. There were a lot of risks. She could have freaked out and reported him, though he had correctly judged that she wasn't that kind of girl. Had she not wanted to do it she would have simply refused.

There was also the risk of being found out. Visiting a teacher in his private residence, let alone to undress and lie in front of him for two hours, would probably not be considered appropriate conduct at St Christopher's.

Finally the risk of what her parents would say. Sera thought it best not to tell them. It would be easy to get away with it on Friday nights anyway as she was barely ever home then. She could just tell a small fib and imply she was going over to Lois's slightly earlier than usual.

Why have I agreed to this? she thought. But looking at the tall, dark, rugged and brilliant man in front of her, she knew the answer. She wanted him. She had wanted him from the first moment he laid furious eyes upon her and made the outrageous demand that she strip.

This demand - or request - was yet more outrageous. He didn't even have the excuse of being mistaken. He knew who she was and how old she was. And despite everything...

It was the "despite" that had pushed her over the edge to accept him. The fact that despite all better judgement, he needed and wanted her to pose for him.

44

As Mr Marek left, Sera watched him walk down the driveway to his car. Broad shoulders and a powerful looking figure.

She shivered. She had probably let herself in for far more than she realised. Than both of them realised.

8. Sex and shopping

"So you're getting naked for him again? This time for pay?"

Lois couldn't stop laughing about the situation.

Sera felt she had to tell her friend, it was too much to deal with otherwise. She knew she could trust Lois. "But you can't tell Joel. It's not that I mind him knowing, it's just that he won't be able to resist joking about it in class."

Sera could imagine it now. Joel digging to try and unsettle Mr Marek. It would likely work and then there would be hell to pay.

They were in a department store, looking at luxury cosmetics that were way beyond their price range. They would try them on, collect any free samples, then find the shades they liked at a cheaper store. It was busy, being a Saturday afternoon, so the sales assistants were too occupied with the customers who actually had money to care about Lois and Sera.

"Do you actually want to do this, Sera?" Lois was looking at her, genuine concern on her face.

Sera did. Secretly inside, she did. She was trying to kid herself and Lois that she was doing it to help him out, or "for the sake of art". But in reality the thought of being alone with Mr Marek for hours each week gave her a thrill that was exciting as it was terrifying.

Except the naked thing. She would much prefer it if he wanted to paint her clothed, but at the end of the day he had already seen her unclothed.

"I guess so."

"Don't let him push you into it. You don't have to do this. I mean if they found out at St Christopher's he'd be sacked before he could pack up his paintbrushes." Lois was trying on an iridescent eye shadow.

"Do you think I shouldn't do it? I like that colour, it looks like beetles' wings. You should get it," Sera told her.

Lois frowned. "Not at eighteen quid. I'll see if my sister can source me some at trade price. Anyway, back to Mr Marek and his request. It's what it might lead to that I think you should think about."

Sera tested a lipstick against the back of her hand. She would need to see it in daylight to know if it worked with her skin or not, the lighting in shops was always deceptive. "What do you mean?"

"He obviously found your body... artistic. I guess with your hair you sort of do look like those Pre-Raphaelite women. Not so ginger maybe," Lois said quickly, seeing Sera bristle. Sera was adamant that her hair was strawberry blonde not red or carrots, since she got a lot of teasing for being "ginger". "But you know what I mean. It's just that given your massive crush on him, and the way that artists are with their models, well..." she tailed off.

"I do not have a massive crush on him," Sera protested.

"You do. Or a little crush, anyway. I mean who wouldn't? I almost do, and I only ever go for blond guys." This was true. Lois admitted to being totally shallow when it came to men, having only one physical type she truly liked. They needed to look like George Peppard in Breakfast at Tiffany's or she was never seriously interested. "Just be careful. I don't want to see you get used or hurt."

Sera inwardly shivered. Thinking about Mr Marek - his strong build, his masculine but sensuous lips - she wouldn't mind him using her in certain ways. Even though she didn't have a lot of experience with that yet. Not like Lois, who had lost her virginity the day it was legal and never looked back.

"I expect he'll be strictly professional. You've seen what he's like in class," Sera pointed out.

Lois was silent for a moment, then grinned. "I guess if nothing else we're in store for some interesting drama. But I demand updates."

"Only if you promise not to tell Joel. Yet, anyway."

"I promise. Your wicked little secret is safe with me."

* * *

For the rest of the week Sera's apprehension grew.

Mr Marek said nothing to her about it in school and she started to wonder if he had changed his mind. Or even if she had imagined the whole thing.

"Something's up with you," Joel said, ever perceptive.

"There's nothing up with me," Sera told him. For the moment it was true.

Joel scrutinised her. They were sketching a taxidermy fox that day. Some ancient samples of butterflies in glass cases had been dredged up from a dusty cupboard in the science lab. A long-forgotten biology teacher had collected them, along with the fox.

Most students had been too squeamish to sit before the stuffed fox with its weird frozen stare so it ended up on the table shared by Joel, Lois and Sera.

"I wish we had the butterflies," Lois said. "The fur or hair on this thing is impossible."

Joel wasn't letting it drop. "There's something you're not telling me."

"I'm just getting some grief at home which is stressing me out," Sera said. This wasn't exactly a lie as she often had stress with her parents, everyone did.

"Marisa?"

"Marisa." The others knew Sera's stepmother all too well.

Mr Marek came to review their progress at that moment, and the subject was dropped.

* * *

At the end of evening class that week Mr Marek finally spoke to her again. The usual people were in the Norfolk Arms once again, Jasper regaling everyone with his scandalous theatrical stories.

As everyone left Mr Marek stopped Sera. "I'll give you a lift."

She guessed that he wanted to speak to her so didn't protest. It was drizzling which at least gave the weather as an excuse.

Jasper overheard and gave Sera a knowing wink. He enjoyed finding any opportunity to stir the pot, he was like Joel in that regard. "We'll see you both next Thursday, then." He put a very subtle emphasis on "both" which Sera noticed, and hoped that Mr Marek hadn't. He was striding ahead of her to the car so hopefully hadn't.

Once again he opened the door for her before getting into the driver's seat. Sera was completely on edge. What if he had changed his mind? She would be both relieved and disappointed.

"Are you still set for Saturday?" he asked.

"Yes."

"I'll drive you past my place now so you can see where it is. If you need me to pick you up, just let me know."

Sera told him she would be fine. She preferred to make her own way there, it avoided awkward questions if her father or Marisa saw his car. Or Mrs Carstairs, their horribly nosey, curtain-twitching neighbour.

"Do I need to wear or bring anything specific?" she asked. She still had a tiny hope that perhaps he would want to draw her clothed. If not, was she supposed to bring her own robe? Did artists just have various ones lying around for their models to use?

He turned to her as he waited at traffic lights and flicked his eyes over her, extinguishing that hope. "Nothing, just come as you are."

Sera swallowed. Her lips felt dry and she longed to put lip balm on them, but although she had some in her bag, she didn't like to do so in front of Mr Marek.

His place was in a relatively easy part of town to get to, it was just east of the centre. A ten minute walk from the bus stop, she calculated.

"Number twenty-seven. Next to the one with the boat," he pointed out. From the look of the boat, on a trailer draped in tarpaulin that was covered with a thick layer of leaves, it looked as though it was rarely moved. Sera wondered if Mr Marek owned the house or was leasing it.

He drove back around the block and headed in the direction of Sera's house. What if he hadn't dropped her off that first time? Would he have approached her somewhere else with his request? What if her parents had been there when he showed up? Sera was running through many different scenarios in her mind.

At her house he stopped the car. "I thought you might have had second thoughts."

It was a challenge rather than an observation. He was daring her not to have them.

"No, it's all good." It wasn't, it was terrifying. But she was determined to see this through.

Before letting her out of the car he reached for a piece of paper and scribbled something down. "Here's my number. Any problems, just let me know." His fingers brushed hers briefly as he handed it to her, and a shock ran up her arm. She bit her lip and looked up at him but couldn't make out his expression. It was intense, that much at least.

Mr Marek opened the door for her and once more she went inside, feeling his eyes burning on her back as she walked up the path to the front door. Less than twenty-four hours to D-day. Drawing day. Being drawn day.

9. On his couch

Sera was increasingly amazed that she had managed to ever undress before a roomful of people.

As the hour drew near for her to pose for Mr Marek - just one artist, in the privacy of his own studio - she was getting increasingly nervous. She had barely eaten all week from the stress, so at least her stomach felt flatter.

She approached number twenty-seven, noticing that the neighbours' unused boat was named Catalina and the house on the other side was subdivided since there were letterboxes marked twenty-five A and twenty-five B. Absorbing these small details kept her grounded. She didn't have to think about what lay ahead.

One minute at a time. Just think about it one minute at a time. You'll get through this, she told herself. *Courage.* She had already downed a couple of glasses of Marisa's Chardonnay to try and steel her nerves.

Sera rang the doorbell, desperately hoping that the art teacher had forgotten or changed his mind or had an emergency and wouldn't answer.

But the door opened.

"Sera." Mr Marek appeared glad and just slightly surprised - relieved? - to see her. "Come in." He was wearing casual trousers and a linen shirt that had traces of paint on the hem.

She wasn't the kind of girl who chickened out. Somehow, this felt like a war. She wished he didn't always look so attractive. If only he were Mr Billings. But then she would have never agreed to pose for Mr Billings, not that he would ever have asked.

"I hope I'm not late." She was pretty certain she wasn't, but she had forgotten to put her watch on.

"You're perfectly on time. Early, in fact."

He took her through the house to his studio, which was out the back in a kind of conservatory or sunroom. It was happily warm in there, she could see a heater positioned near a chaise longue-style couch draped with some rich-coloured fabric. *You and I*, Sera thought to the couch, *are going to survive this together.* She remembered Mr Marek's words about "arranging her on his couch" and suppressed a shiver.

What might he try when they were all alone?

"I was lucky to find this house, having this room attached. The light is perfect," he told her.

It was true, the wintry sunlight lit up the room, but without shining directly onto the area in which he had positioned the couch and easel. A few plants in pots were situated around the edges of the room, some yucca and others that Sera didn't recognise.

"You haven't lived here long?" she asked.

"Just a couple of months." He saw her looking at the plants. "Those came with the house. I've done what I can to water them, but they've seen better days."

Sera noticed that Mr Marek didn't elaborate as to where he had lived before, but she assumed it was in London.

It was now or never. "Shall I...?" Sera had no clue exactly how to put this. Disrobe? Undress? Get ready? Get into position? There didn't seem to be a single phrase that didn't carry some huge innuendo. If she didn't have such a stupid crush on him it would probably be much easier.

"If you're happy getting started straight away." He hesitated. "Normally I'd offer you a drink but given your age and the fact we're already on thin ice, I think it would be unwise. Would you like a tea or coffee?"

"Just water, thanks." Her throat felt so dry she could barely articulate the words.

"Great. You can use the study to change."

Mr Marek went out to the kitchen and Sera went through the other door, which opened off the conservatory on the opposite side. The room reminded her of a theatre set: French windows and doors off different walls. She was going to be the star performer.

There was a hat stand which she used to hang up her coat, folding the rest of her clothes on a chair. A clean dressing gown was draped over the back of the chair, the white kind that you got in hotel rooms. Sera glanced at it and wasn't surprised to see a prominent hospitality chain logo.

She had brought her own robe but put on the one that he had left out for her. Braced herself. This was it.

* * *

Taking a deep breath, Sera re-entered the conservatory and made her way straight to the couch. She didn't look right or left because she didn't want to catch his eye and lose her nerve.

"So what do I do?" she asked. She noticed a muscle clench in his jaw and hoped she hadn't annoyed him. But what did he expect? She was entirely new to this, unless you counted the ten unplanned minutes at the community centre.

"If the room feels warm enough, you can get into position. Remember how you were last time? We'll try something similar to that. I'll be making a few sketches until the positioning looks right, so this afternoon is more for getting that right."

Sera ran her tongue over her lips nervously. She sipped the water he had offered her, hoping it would ease the dryness in her mouth. She wanted to close her eyes but instead she cast them down to the floor, said a silent prayer to the gods of painting, and slipped off the robe.

For a moment the silence was so thick you could have cut the air with a knife. She didn't dare look at Mr Marek.

To her horror, despite the warmth of the room, she felt her nipples harden as a reaction to being exposed to air. She prayed once more to the art gods that he wouldn't notice.

Then, trying to manoeuvre herself as gracefully as possible, Sera lay down on the couch. At least her behind was hidden. And lying down made her stomach nice and flat - almost concave, even.

Finally she looked up and caught his eyes, seeing the amusement there and something she couldn't quite discern. Was it sympathy?

The thought that he might pity her in some way was a wake up call. Sera steeled her nerves and raised her chin slightly. She could meet any challenge.

"That's great." His voice was carefully neutral. "Arm along the back again. This couch is a different shape, hold on." He fetched a small velvet cushion from the floor and wedged it behind her neck and shoulder, raising her head. It was hard and Sera felt twisted. She wriggled to try and get comfortable again. "That works," Mr Marek said. "I'll probably only need twenty minutes like this, then we can switch. Just let me know if and when you need a break. I realise you're not used to this."

He flicked his eyes across her body as he said this, and for a moment Sera felt vulnerable and strangely passive. Then his professional detachment seemed to return, and Sera became a human bowl-of-fruit once again.

There was silence as he started to work but it wasn't an easy one. At least on Sera's part. It felt like the tension in the room was growing and growing, and for all this was supposed to be twenty minutes it felt like two hours.

She barely dared look at him, just flicking her eyes to him occasionally. Most of the time he seemed absorbed in his work. Which was her, of course. Her naked body.

Sera swallowed. She really wasn't sure how she was going to manage this week after week.

Then he spoke, breaking the silence.

"This is working well, I think this will be the pose we'll use. First time lucky. We'll try it more upright in a moment, but this seems to be about right. Is it comfortable enough for you to hold it?"

Physically, kind of. Mentally, no. Sera wished she had downed the whole bottle of Chardonnay because the effects of the couple of glasses had soon worn off.

"It's fine." She wasn't going to admit the truth.

Mr Marek smiled and it made her feel dizzy. "Great. You're warm enough?"

"Perfect."

"Perfect?" He turned it into a question and she flushed. "You do look pretty perfect from here."

It was an explicit compliment, such a shock that Sera was sure her skin flamed fiery red.

Then he qualified it, leaving her unsure as to whether or not she had read too much into it. "The lighting is just right, and the form."

He got her to sit more upright for the second sketch. Sera was just hugely relieved the pose wasn't any more revealing. She had seen enough examples of life drawing to know that every angle was frequently explored. And while she didn't have an issue with nudity in art, some of the more gynaecological poses were rather confronting.

If he asked to pose like that - legs akimbo - she honestly wasn't sure that she could have managed it.

Fortunately he didn't. To her surprise, he even spoke to her as he worked. "Have you always lived here?"

"All my life, yes," Sera told him. Then worried that this would make her seem a dull, small town girl. "This will be my last year though, before hopefully going to London."

"Saint Martins?"

"If I get accepted."

Mr Marek picked up another charcoal. "I doubt you'll have a problem with that."

Sera decided to be bold. "So what brought you here? You mentioned your parents retired here?" She remembered he had said his mother was dead and hoped her question wasn't inappropriate.

He didn't look away from his easel, making what appeared to be swift shading lines. His movements were deft and masterful, there was nothing tentative about his strokes. "A sick and elderly father who requires more care than he is willing to accept."

"He doesn't live here with you?"

"He's lived in a one-bedroom flat for some years and won't budge. My job for the year - other than teaching art - is to manoeuvre him into suitable retirement accommodation," Mr Marek said.

Sera was surprised he had revealed this much. "How old is he?"

"Nearly eighty." He sat back from his drawing, appraising it. Sera burned with curiosity to see how he had drawn her, and also dreaded to see it if it looked ugly. Or worse... revealing. "Nearly eighty and as stubborn as a mule."

Sera couldn't resist. "Do you take after him?"

The art teacher cast her a direct glance. "If you mean do I insist on getting my way, then yes."

"Some battles ahead, then." She could just imagine the two men locking their figurative horns, as the son strove to get the father out of his home and somewhere safer for him.

"Some considerable battles." His tone was cool but not annoyed. He put down his charcoal. "That's done. And yes, I prefer the first position. Even if you look considerably less like a frightened virgin in this one."

Sera was mortified.

If she had blushed pink before and then red, she was certainly a deep shade of beetroot now. There was no hiding it.

Mr Marek looked at her, amusement and a shade of remorse mingling in his expression as he saw her embarrassment. "Good God, are you still...?" He left the question open while Sera died a thousand deaths.

Yes, she was. And she wasn't really sure why, she just was. He was probably going to assume she was uptight and inhibited, but it was more a series of accidents and delays and - if she was going to be honest - there never having been anyone in town that looked like Mr Marek.

At least now she had met him, it kind of made sense why she hadn't felt enough inclination to go all the way with any of the previous boys she had dated.

Following this they went back to silence. Sera was too frozen with mortification to say anything. Mr Marek perhaps realised he had crossed a line. After all, she was his student. His professional detachment returned and he got her to pose in a couple more ways before calling it a day.

After Sera had hurriedly dressed herself again, which felt like putting on much-missed armour, Mr Marek offered to drive Sera home. She declined as she wanted the walk to clear her head. "Thank you for coming. It really did go well, so I hope you'll be able to continue," he told her.

Just as she was exiting the front door when he told her to wait, and extended a white envelope. "Your professional fee."

Sera almost wanted to reject it, feeling like a complete amateur, but she was struck by the grace and respect with which he handed it to her. She met his eyes, and for a split second they were equals, before all the circumstances swam around her again. Teacher, student. Artist, model. Worldly, inexperienced.

It was a gulf too wide to bridge. Even if Sera was starting to associate the aroma of charcoal and oil paint with a pair of slate grey eyes and the ardent desire for his lips on hers.

10. Still wary

"You told him you were a virgin?!"

Lois couldn't stop laughing.

Sera protested. "No! I didn't tell him anything. I didn't even say anything."

"But you basically let him guess, right? If you say nothing, and just go red, that's obviously what he's going to think." Lois and Sera had gone out for sushi before hitting a few bars. It was the first restaurant in town to have food going round on a conveyor belt, which made it such a novelty that it was always packed.

Lois reached out towards a plate with three exquisitely arranged pieces of rice and seaweed, then hovered over another one with two larger sushi on it. "Which costs more, green plates or red ones? Oh who cares, I'll eat both anyway." She took both plates and picked up her chopsticks again. "Anyway, I told you it was becoming a millstone. You'll be like one of these women that waits and waits and eventually has to join a nunnery because everything has sealed up from lack of use."

Sera ignored her and unscrewed the cap from a tiny plastic fish containing soy sauce. "I'm not holding on to it, necessarily. I just haven't met anyone whom I've been tempted enough to make the leap with."

"Until a certain art teacher unpacked his brushes?"

Once again Sera refused to respond. "It's not like there's any rush. We don't get tested for it at A-levels, do we?"

Lois was silent for a moment, toying with some sliced ginger. "Just imagine that. If we did all get tested. I wonder what would be a pass and what would be a fail? Or imagine if you got sent to a specific university based on the results?"

Sera really didn't want to imagine this. While she wasn't intimately acquainted with all of her classmates' sexual histories, she didn't particularly want to be grouped among the undateables. The thought of being sent to a remote University of Virgins in the wilds of Scotland or somewhere was chilling. Perhaps Lois was right and she should just get rid of it quickly.

A group of guys entered and took seats further long the bench. They immediately started giving Lois and Sera a subtle eyeing up. Sera briefly imagined just hooking up with one of them, getting it all over with.

But they just seemed so insubstantial. So much less rugged and virile than... She forced herself to stop thinking about him and tried to focus on her food.

But Lois persisted.

"Honestly, I'd kill to be a fly on the wall," she said. "You lying there in the buff with Mr Marek cracking jokes about your prudishness."

"He didn't crack a joke and I wasn't prudish."

"You said it was really awkward though," Lois pointed out.

"Well it was. You try lying there, stark naked, in front of someone that...."

"...someone that you have a massive crush on?" Lois teased. "Maybe you should get him to give you a bit of extra education. He paid you for the session, didn't he? Maybe you could take payment in kind. Private biology lessons in return for modelling."

The thought of ever putting such an absurd proposition to Mr Marek was so horrifying that Sera couldn't speak.

Horrifying, yet amazingly, amazingly...

"You're actually thinking about it, aren't you?" Lois said. "I'm sure there are worse options. At least he'd know what he was doing. He looks like he's a man of the world, if you know what I mean."

Sera knew exactly what Lois meant.

They had both been impressed with the amount of money Sera had been paid for the session. They'd previously had no idea of what models actually received so Lois had made some inquiries. When Sera finally opened the envelope, they calculated that Mr

Marek had paid her about twenty per cent above the average rate for a two hour life class. Pretty generous.

"You still have all that money to spend," Lois reminded her. "And more to come next week, presumably."

The money was burning a hole in Sera's purse. Somehow it felt wrong, as though she hadn't earned it properly. She tried to explain this to Lois, who rolled her eyes.

"You earned every penny. Give it to me if you're so hung up with guilt about it. It's not like you earned it for selling drugs or something, is it? Or on the game?"

The problem was that this latter was very much what it did feel like. Being paid for her body rather than her mind. Except if she were on the game, Mr Marek would expect her to do more than just lie there. And he certainly wouldn't be keeping any professional distance.

Sera shivered. If she was ever going to sell her body, she knew exactly who she would want the buyer to be.

* * *

Jasper had discovered that Elizabeth sang in a folk band, and had decided the whole class should attend her next performance to support her. This was taking place in a traditional country pub a few miles out of town.

Elizabeth was pleased but very flustered. "Oh no, really, there's no need to come. I realise that folk music is hardly fashionable these days."

"Nonsense. It's part of a long and well respected musical tradition, dating back over the centuries. You're preserving our heritage, Elizabeth dear." Jasper trilled a few bars of Greensleeves and Sera tried not to giggle.

"A cousin of mine used to play folk music. He was a Morris dancer," said Winfred, who was sipping a small sherry. Jasper had finally managed to persuade both Bob and Winifred to join them in the Norfolk Arms, so the entire class was there that night.

Including their teacher.

It was strange. On one hand Sera and Mr Marek shared this huge secret and she sensed a reluctant bond with him over it. On

60

the other hand he was clearly trying to put up the biggest wall of formality between them at all other times.

She still cringed to think of him discovering her virginity. It was bad enough that he already thought she was too young, being underage. Though thankfully he hadn't made any more comments about her coming to the Norfolk Arms and drinking alcohol.

Besides, she would be eighteen in just a few weeks. A legal adult.

Sera glanced at Mr Marek and as if he sensed her eyes on him, he met her gaze. She felt a weird flip in her stomach. If only everyone else knew, she thought. What would they think? Jasper already made the odd hint and innuendo. She wasn't sure whether it was just random teasing on his part or whether he had picked up on the suppressed chemistry between her and their art teacher.

Jasper set down his tankard with a light thump.

"So it's settled then. We'll all be there, in our finest."

"It's really a very casual affair," Elizabeth said. "Just a country pub. I shouldn't worry about dressing up." She looked anxious and Sera imagined she was probably picturing Jasper striding into the Green Man Inn wearing a top hat and tails.

"Subdued finery it shall be then," Jasper promised.

Sera was glad at his lightening the mood, because the tension she felt towards the dark, chiselled man across the table was so intense that she was sure everyone else must be sensing it.

Bob got up to buy the next round of drinks. "I'll certainly look forward to it," he said, rubbing his beard. He turned to Sera. "You catch the bus normally, don't you? If you need a lift, just let me know. I'll be picking up Winifred and there'll be plenty of room."

"Thank you." Sera was surprised and grateful for the offer. She could have borrowed Marisa's or her father's car, but this way she could enjoy a couple of drinks.

Mr Marek was the only person who hadn't yet confirmed his attendance. Jasper tactfully addressed this.

"You may already have commitments, of course, but should you be available I can offer you a map. The roads out that way are a labyrinth of narrow country lanes and hedges, it's easy to miss the turn off."

"I'll be there." The art teacher didn't indicate whether he would need help with directions, but his tone was polite.

He would be there... of course this prospect transformed the whole occasion in Sera's head.

"What do you sing?" she asked Elizabeth. "I'm afraid I don't know a lot of folk music."

Elizabeth smiled. She was wearing her usual dangly earrings - this evening they had tiny turquoise and bronze beads, picking out the vivid colours in the printed scarf she wore wound about her neck. "You'll probably find you recognise a few of the songs. We do a version of Puff the Magic Dragon and several other contemporary tunes."

Sera had heard of Puff the Magic Dragon at least.

"I've always liked that one about Bangor," Barry said.

"That's a very jolly song," Winifred agreed.

Elizabeth said they didn't currently perform it but she would look at adding to their repertoire.

Sera knew the song and suddenly had a vision of sitting in a pub with Mr Marek listening to Elizabeth's band cheerfully singing about what a lovely time they had on a day trip to Bangor. The image was so incongruous she wanted to laugh. It was a bit of a leap from The Retro to 1970s folk music. She had no idea what he normally listened to as no music had been playing at his home, but she was sure he didn't own Fiddler's Dram's Greatest Hits.

She would have much preferred to spend time with him in a dark bar again rather than a country pub on a Sunday afternoon. To dance with him again, without anyone else around who knew them. She was sure he would put up less resistance a second time, maybe even take the lead.

Mr Marek's eyes were on her again and Sera desperately hoped he couldn't read her mind. If only she could read his. Despite visiting him in his own home and lying naked before him, he remained the most mysterious man she had ever met.

11. Shocking words

The second modelling session started better than the first. Sera felt much less terrified though she still was far from relaxed.

Once again she undressed in the study, put on the white robe - freshly laundered, she noticed - and took her place on the couch.

"All set?" Mr Marek asked her.

Sera, suddenly finding her voice frozen in her throat, nodded and the art teacher picked up a pencil.

He was starting the actual painting this week and Sera was a little taken aback at the size of canvas he had chosen. It was huge. She had some idea of how much large canvases cost and hoped her image would be worth the expenditure.

Still, he could always paint over it with something else if he needed to. Idly Sera imagined art experts centuries in the future managing to view the "hidden" image beneath the top layer of paint, as happened with Old Masters. Using modern technology they often found earlier versions of the final painting that had been painted over, or even discovered entirely different works long-buried beneath.

She hoped they wouldn't judge her appearance too harshly. She imagined them joking about "no wonder she was painted over" and then feared that people in her own time might well say the same.

A shadow must have passed over her face because Mr Marek asked: "Is anything wrong?"

"Nothing, I was just thinking about the canvas size," Sera said.

"The canvas size?"

"That you could always paint over it again, if you need to. Reuse it."

Mr Marek put down the brush he had been holding. He looked directly at her, his face serious. "Trust me, Sera, I won't ever be painting over this. Ever."

"You don't ever reuse canvases?" Sera asked.

"Rarely. But this work will never be painted over. So if you think your efforts or mine will be wasted, you can be assured that they won't."

Sera felt bad for having even thought this now and was silent. She lay there, trying to remain calm and still as he worked on the painting.

After what felt like around ten minutes, Mr Marek swore. "It's not right. You don't look the same."

Sera was bewildered. "I haven't changed anything."

"It's the look in your eye, from that first time in the life class. It's not there," he told her.

"What look?"

Mr Marek was silent for a moment. Then he spoke, his voice huskier.

"You know what look."

How had she looked that first time? Sera remembered being angry and feeling defiant. Wanting to embarrass him more than he had embarrassed her.

He came and knelt down by her. Murmured in her ear. "Like you wanted me to fuck you."

Sera gasped, shocked.

Had he really just said that?

Her art teacher had accused her of wanting her to... she could barely rethink the words.

His proximity was doing things to her body she couldn't control. Making her feel hot all over her skin. She could feel her nipples grow hard and prayed he wouldn't notice.

But his eyes never left her face. "And knowing full well that I want to fuck you senseless."

Her eyes widened and then half closed at the image of it.

"That's the look." He was satisfied. "Hold those thoughts."

"You want to have sex with me?"

Mr Marek smiled, a slow, lazy smile. He leant nearer. "I want to run my hands over every part of your body, force your legs

64

apart and screw you until you are begging me to stop and begging for more," he told her. "But I'm not going to lay a single finger on you. Instead you're going to lie there and imagine it, and give me the expression I need for my work."

Lie there and imagine having sex with him? Sera shivered involuntarily. She had spent enough effort trying not to think of that scenario.

He was so close to her that she could almost taste what it would be like if he kissed her. His lips... the clean male smell of his skin... the shadow of stubble, he hadn't shaved that day.

But he stood up, and ran his eyes over her body in a lingering way. There was no professional detachment in his gaze right now. It was raw, sexual appreciation and Sera felt her body react despite her attempts to stay calm.

"Absolutely perfect." Mr Marek drew the words out, a faint smile on his lips and a glint of triumph in his eyes. He had her exactly where he wanted her. He had warned her last time that he always got what he wanted, and now Sera was beginning to understand what he meant by that.

* * *

Mr Marek didn't try to make conversation after that but worked from behind his easel while Sera lay on the couch, her emotions in turmoil.

She felt embarrassed, aroused, frustrated. She wanted him desperately. Now he had mentioned touching her body she couldn't get the thought of it out of her head.

I want to run my hands over every part of your body...

She wanted to do the same. Feel his lean muscles, twist her finger in his thick, dark hair where it rose from the nape of his neck. He had recently had it cut short at the back, revealing the strong contours of the back of his neck, down to his broad and powerful shoulders.

Sera was also wondering if he had meant what he said. Did her art teacher really want to screw her, or were these things he just said to get models in the right mood?

If so it was pretty ruthless. But then he was ruthless, wasn't he? She remembered how Mr Marek had reacted in both her first life drawing class and when he had realised she was also his school student.

Getting involved with him probably would be playing with fire.

But she wanted to be burned...

Briefly she closed her eyes, only to be startled by a sharp command. "Don't fall asleep!"

As if she could do that. Lying at a weird angle on the couch without moving was hardly comfortable, even if it was a very large and spacious couch.

"I'm wide awake."

"Good, because you wouldn't enjoy my method of waking you up." His gaze seared into hers for a moment and she was tempted to try it, to test him. To pretend to doze off so he would be forced to come and wake her. Maybe with a kiss, Sleeping Beauty style?

"It involves cold water," Mr Marek said, disillusioning her. Sera hoped he hadn't read her mind.

"You could just call out," she said.

He gave a taunting smile. "Cold water has other advantages."

"Such as?"

"It perks things up, should they need it." His eyes ran along her body suggestively.

"They won't need it," Sera told him, trying to maintain her composure.

"So I can see."

Once again her traitorous body was responding to his words and the tone of her voice. She tried to force it to feel normal. But every nerve, every cell was aware of the tall, dark man just a few feet away. It was infuriating that he obviously knew it. So much for wearing one's heart on one's sleeve: she didn't even have a sleeve. And more than her heart was giving things away.

"Do your models usually fall asleep on you?" Sera asked. What she wanted to ask was whether this was how he normally spoke to his models, but didn't want to ask directly.

"Not so far. But then I rarely paint figures," he told her. "Teaching the life class at the Community Centre is something of a diversion. Naturally I've studied life drawing, but it's not my main discipline."

Sera was curious. "So what is?"

Mr Marek glanced at his watch. "We're pretty much done here for today. Get dressed, and I'll show you."

Sera scrambled into the robe and pulled her clothes on in the adjacent room as quickly as possible, before rejoining him in the studio. He led her through the kitchen to a living room the other side.

"There."

It was a seascape: a huge, powerful, stormy, angry sea. Dark green, indigo, grey and cobalt waves tossed a fragile craft around under a howling sky. Greys and blacks were cut with flashes of white while a strange, sinister amber gilded the edges of the clouds.

Sera couldn't speak for a few moments, absorbing the painting. Its fury, its brilliance.

Then she turned to him. "A self-portrait?"

For a second Mr Marek froze. Something flared in his eyes: not exactly anger, but a dark emotion that died away almost as instantly as it had appeared.

When he spoke his voice was calm. "Partly."

Sera was flooded with relief. She had no idea what had inspired her to say that to him. Given how ominous and violent the painting was, it could hardly be construed as a compliment. Yet she had been right.

"When did you paint it?"

"Four years and three months ago." His eyes were locked on hers.

"And you haven't painted anything since?" Once again Sera had no idea how she knew this nor why she couldn't stop her mouth from blabbing it.

He winced. "Correct."

As Sera broke the gaze to look once more at the painting, Mr Marek spoke again.

"Until you."

12. Keeping his distance

"Remember what I told you last week?" The mocking glint was back in Mr Marek's eye as Sera lay on his couch once again.

How could she forget? "Yes."

"I want that expression again from you." The art teacher was just behind the couch, rearranging the folds of the drape as they had been before. As ever, Sera felt on edge and hyper-aware of his proximity.

Despite the effect he had on her, she wasn't sure if she could just drum it up on cue. "Those things you said last week..."

Mr Marek stopped and leant down to her. "Would you like me to say them again?" His voice was low, taunting her.

That wasn't what she was trying to ask. "Did you actually mean them?" Was he just toying with her, winding her up to get what he wanted, or did he actually want to do those things to her as well?

He laughed. "Do I want to screw you? What do you reckon?"

Sera wasn't sure. "I didn't know if you were just saying it all."

"It doesn't matter whether I meant it or not, because I'm not going to lay a finger on you. You're underage, you're my student, and I want you exactly as you are for this painting."

He drew out the words "exactly as you are". She guessed he was referring to her virginity and felt humiliated.

Mr Marek saw her expression change. He moved his lips closer to her ear; she could feel the heat of his breathing by her neck. "But yes, Sera, I'm still a man. I have a young, naked, woman before me. Were it not for the fact I intend to paint you, I would like nothing more than to fuck you senseless."

Sera tried to breathe normally and not let him see the effect his words and his closeness had on her. She was pretty sure he could tell.

He dropped his voice. "And knowing that I would be your first..."

Sera caught her breath. There was nothing more she wanted in that moment than for Mr Marek to be her first. "Couldn't we?"

Please touch me. Make me yours. She didn't say out loud but it was written all over her.

But he stood up and looked down at her. "We could, but we're not going to. Not now or ever, for the reasons I've just outlined."

Sera wanted to protest. It was so unfair: him tormenting her like this, knowing full well what it did to her. "I'll be eighteen next week." It hardly made sense to wait seven more days. It was already legal.

"Not next week, Sera. Not next month, nor next year. I'm not screwing one of my pupils. But if imagining it gives you the exact expression you have now, then please hold that thought."

She couldn't think of much else when she was lying in his presence with her clothes off, watching him as he worked. His dark hair fell over his forehead and she longed to push it back. Every time he looked back at her from the easel she longed for him to change his mind, to break his resolve.

Mr Marek returned to his easel and Sera lay on the couch, once again burning with frustration and unassuaged desire.

There was silence for some time which made Sera aware of all the smaller noises around them. A lone bird outside in the wintry garden. The faint hum of the electric fire. The ticking of a clock she couldn't see. The occasional scrape of his palette knife or creak of his chair as he shifted. Her own breathing, which she tried to quieten as it seemed to echo through the room.

Then a loud, shrill ringing.

The telephone.

Mr Marek frowned. "I'll have to get it. Very few people have this number, so..."

So it might be important, even an emergency. Sera understood.

Wondering if she should have taken the opportunity to stand up and stretch while he was out of the room, Sera lay there waiting. A minute later Mr Marek returned from the hallway. "It was the hospital. My father has had a fall. I'm afraid I'll have to cut our session short today."

* * *

Mr Marek insisted on paying Sera in full, with the usual envelope, and she insisted on not just leaving him.

"Parking at the hospital is a nightmare, you can drive round for ages when the carparks are full. At least let me park your car for you."

She was surprised at how quickly he acquiesced. He was clearly very shaken: she hoped it wasn't a life or death situation.

On the way there Sera tried to find something encouraging to say. "At least if he's already in hospital, he's in the best hands." It sounded horribly clichéd, but so did everything in these kind of circumstances.

They pulled up just outside Emergency, Sera having directed him to take the quickest route to the hospital, and then she got into the driver's seat to try to find a car space. As predicted it wasn't easy: the main car park was full up, as always. It was supposed to be for short stay only but Sera suspected many of the cars were left there all day.

The long stay car park and the overspill area across the road were also both packed. There were other cars circling around hoping for a spot. In the end Sera drove to a "No Parking" area behind a nearby block of flats. She knew it wasn't monitored by parking wardens because a friend of Joel's had once lived there.

Then she walked back to the main entrance hospital to return Mr Marek's keys, planning to try and leave them at reception for him with a note before catching a bus home.

But when she walked through the doors, he was waiting for her. His face looked worried but not grief stricken so she presumed the worst hadn't happened so far.

"Sera. Thank you so much."

"How is your father? Have you seen him?"

"He's in surgery, he hit his head when he fell. They seem to think he'll pull through."

Sera smiled with relief for him. "That's good to hear."

"You should get going, you've done enough for me already," Mr Marek told her.

He looked suddenly exhausted and Sera was reluctant to leave him. She felt a weird kind of role reversal where she was finally the one with more experience, in a position to help. She knew the hospital, the area. A few of her parents' social circle even worked here: an orthopaedic surgeon, a haematologist, an obstetric nurse. All very useful contacts if you needed insider help.

Whereas Mr Marek was the stranger in town.

"You sit down in case they call you, I'll get you a coffee from the vending machine," she offered.

He reached for some change and Sera tried to refuse it - after all it was only a quid or so - but he insisted.

At the machine she realised that she had no clue how he took his coffee. She guessed black and grabbed a couple of sachets of sugar and a stirrer.

"Thanks. You didn't get one for yourself?"

She hadn't even thought of it, she had expected he would want her to leave him once she had brought him his. But instead he held out a coin. "Here."

Surprised, Sera went to get herself a drink from the machine as well: a second cup of hot dark brown water. She took a seat across from him on one of the rows of plastic chairs that were fixed to the floor.

They sat there in silence for what seemed like ages. Although Mr Marek didn't speak to her, Sera sensed that he needed her there. It wasn't personal - anyone would have done, she was sure - it was just having the presence of someone else to keep company. To keep a vigil.

The minutes ticked by. A quarter of an hour, then half. Sera was getting increasingly nervous that no news was bad news when a nurse came up to them. Her face looked calm but not necessarily encouraging.

Sera dug her nails into her palms, mentally willing the update to be hopeful.

"Mr Marek?" He looked up and the nurse's face brightened. "Your father is through surgery and is currently stable. The doctor will speak further with you, but so far everything looks well."

The relief in the art teacher's eyes moved Sera. A weight of dread had been lifted from him: the tension left his shoulders.

"When can I see him?" Mr Marek asked.

"He's still in recovery right now, but once they move him to the intensive care ward you'll be able to make a short visit. They'll probably want to keep him under observation for a few days."

The nurse went off to speak with the receptionist and Sera and Mr Marek were left together once more.

"I'm so glad," Sera said. She meant it sincerely.

"Likewise." He paused, looking at her. "And thank you for being here."

The way he looked at her, even though it was only gratitude, made her stomach flip.

"It's no problem. I'll get going now as you'll be going to see him."

"If you stay I'll give you a lift back."

It was a tempting thought, but Sera felt that she would be in the way. Mr Marek might want to spend longer with his father or talking to the doctors. He might want to gather his thoughts. Whatever the case, he'd have enough on his plate without the hassle of having to drive her across town.

"Truly it's okay. I'll see you next week. And if there's anything I can do, just let me know."

"I will," he promised, and Sera left.

13. A birthday surprise

Sera had finally told Lois about some of the things Mr Marek had said to her, though not about the visit to the hospital. She felt that was his private business.

Typically, Lois had been amused rather than shocked by his explicit talk. "You'll both have to get it out of your system at some point," she told Sera.

But when? How?

"You have to break down his resolve. Find the chink in his armour." Unfortunately Lois had no more idea than Sera as to what Mr Marek's Achilles heel might be.

"It's not as though I can wear something sexy or revealing, because, you know," Sera said.

Lois laughed. "Given he's already gazed upon your naked form for hours on end and managed to resist you, I guess not. Unless you flash just a little bit more. I take it that the pose isn't quite Basic Instinct-level explicit?"

It wasn't, but Sera had no intention of imitating Sharon Stone's infamous vagina-flash. "I'd feel like one of those female baboon monkeys, waving that in his face."

"The ones that swell up all pink when they're in season? Well, if it works for them..." Lois gave a wicked grin.

"Except homo sapiens doesn't have quite the same attributes." Thank God. Imagine being in a nightclub or on the beach in a bikini and that happening in front of some hot guy, Sera thought. It was awkward enough that nipples had a life of their own without your genitals turning into a bright pink balloon. She pointed this out to Lois.

"It's a tough one, isn't it?" Lois said. "What else could you do? Lie there and lick your lips? Touch yourself? Talk dirty back to him?"

Sera could not countenance doing any of these things.

"You know he wants you, so maybe it's not so much about you trying to be more sexy. Maybe it's about making some kind of move when his defences are down. If they're ever down. He always seems to be so in control of everything. At least he is in class," Lois said.

This was true. Compared to poor old Mr Billings, or most of the other teachers at St Christopher's, Mr Marek had absolute command and control of the art class. This was all the more impressive since people tended to relax and mess around in art. But now he was teaching, things were very disciplined.

"Of course he may have a girlfriend already," Sera said. He might even have a fiancée or a wife, she supposed.

"If he does, I doubt she'd be too impressed with your modelling sessions," Lois said. "It's one thing him painting someone, quite another saying all that stuff. Even if they're all Bohemian types I bet she'd be pissed off."

They had to change the subject as Joel arrived. Sera was still feeling guilty for keeping him in the dark. The longer she left it, the harder it was going to be to tell him.

"It's the soon-to-be-birthday girl. What are you planning to do when you wake up tomorrow? Vote? Get married? Have your first ever legal sip of alcohol to toast the end of your youth?" Joel put down a brightly coloured bunch of flowers on the desk, which made Sera feel even worse.

"Thank you, they're beautiful."

"Fight on the front lines. Serve on a jury. Make a will." Joel was still reeling off the list of rights that Sera would gain within the next twenty-four hours.

Lois picked up the flowers and smelled them. "They are lovely. So we're still on for tomorrow night?"

They were going for dinner with a few other people to celebrate Sera's eighteenth, and then nightclubbing. Sera hadn't wanted to have a huge party as she would only spend the whole time stressed about gatecrashers or someone setting the house on fire. Her parents had offered to book her a venue but she preferred the idea of a restaurant.

"Absolutely."

"We should take you out to lunch as well," Joel said. "Or are your parents doing that?"

Sera and Lois met one another's glance, knowing that Saturday lunch time was modelling time. "About that..." Sera began. It seemed like high time to confess.

Joel raised his eyebrows. "Something you haven't told us? A hot date already set up?"

Hot, but not a date. If only.

"There is something. I don't even know why I didn't tell you before. You have to promise to keep your mouth shut though. And from tomorrow I can probably sue you, so be warned." Sera gave him a brief outline of the modelling sessions. She didn't mention the suggestive things that Mr Marek had said.

Fortunately Joel wasn't affronted that he hadn't been told earlier and instead found the situation hilarious. "You just lie there starkers with Marek sketching away?"

"He's painting with oils," Sera told him.

"What's it look like? Has he shown you the work in progress?" Mr Marek hadn't, and Sera hadn't dared to ask him about it. "What if it's a really bizarre style? He might have painted you with a penis or something. You should sneak a peek before it's too late."

"There isn't really a chance to."

Joel turned to Sera. "So let me get this straight. You lie there, and he paints, and nothing else? Despite all that tension between the two of you that should be obvious to anyone with eyes?"

Once again, Sera and Lois shot one another an uneasy glance, which Joel noticed and seized on.

"What? Don't tell me he's some kind of Toulouse Lautrec? Girl with a Pearl Necklace and all that."

"It's Girl with a Pearl Earring," Lois pointed out. "And even I know that Lautrec didn't paint that one."

Joel gave a smirk. "I know what I said. All the great artists screwed their models. So has he deflowered you on his couch? Made you his mistress?"

76

"No, and no. Nothing like that." Sera felt herself going red.

"He talks dirty to her," Lois told Joel.

Joel's mouth fell open at this. He demanded a blow-by-blow account and Sera gave him a somewhat edited one.

"You clearly need to move this on then," Joel told her. "You can't just leave it there."

"That's what I've been telling her," Lois said.

Lois and Joel were clearly going to gang up on Sera about this. She was never going to hear the end of it until she had reported some progress.

"Ask him for a birthday kiss. See what happens."

"Invite him out to have a birthday drink with you."

Sera knew that she would probably not be able to bring herself to do either, but she played along. She could understand why they were so fascinated: she would have been just the same in their shoes. It was hugely forbidden and potentially scandalous, which was why Mr Marek was holding back. Or she assumed that was why, unless he had a girlfriend as well.

But why not try? She had nothing to lose, except the one thing she really wanted to lose.

* * *

Sera loved her birthday. No matter how bad the weather was, or if it fell on a school day, it always felt like her own personal festival.

It started with a special family breakfast where her father cooked bacon and eggs, along with mushrooms, grilled tomatoes and fried bread. The twins always wanted pancakes for their birthday but Sera's favourite was an old fashioned English breakfast.

A long, wonderful day lay ahead: and best of all it was a Saturday. That meant getting to be with Mr Marek for two whole hours, then spending the rest of the evening and night with her friends.

It couldn't be more perfect. Even if Mr Marek had returned to his usual cool detachment during the week, she was looking forward to their session today.

But when he opened the door to her he was clearly in a black mood. "Sera." He barely greeted her.

Sera had a sudden fear that something was wrong with his father. "Is your father still getting better?" she asked. She had briefly inquired as to his condition in the week and had been relieved to hear that he was progressing well.

"He is. They may release him tonight," Mr Marek told her.

"That's great news."

"Leading to an even greater problem. He can't stay by himself any more and he won't accept any home care."

No wonder he was so stressed, Sera thought. "Could he stay here?"

"He refuses to consider living anywhere except his flat."

Sera wondered what old Mr Marek was like. She imagined an elderly, grey haired version of her art teacher, probably as equally as stubborn and strong-willed as his son. "What if you told him it was temporary?"

"The problem is that it's not. His flat is up two flights of stairs with no lift. The occupational therapist says it's no longer appropriate for him to live there."

"But you could imply that it was temporary, couldn't you?" Sera suggested. "Just while he recuperates. Then if he got used to living here, he might more open to..." she trailed off, not wanting to say "an old people's home" in case it sounded too negative.

Mr Marek was silent for a moment. "That could possibly work. He's extremely set in his ways though." He started sorting out some brushes and paints and Sera took it as her cue to change out of her clothes. Getting undressed was starting to feel more routine, though she still felt exposed lying in front of him.

Let alone with him saying all those things to her...

She emerged from the study in the usual robe. "It's my birthday today," she told him.

He looked up, unsmiling. "Many happy returns of the day."

Sera wanted more than a Hallmark greeting from him. She held his gaze. "So I'm now eighteen. Of age." She stressed the last words.

Mr Marek looked directly at her, refusing to rise to the bait. "Congratulations."

Sera summoned up all her courage. She decided to take Lois's and Joel's advice and just go for it.

"Do I get a birthday kiss?"

She let the robe fall around her feet at that moment, managing to give what she hoped was a sultry smile, and was gratified to see him react with a start. He certainly wasn't looking at her like a bowl of fruit today: his eyes were devouring her in quite a different way.

He gritted his teeth. "You're still my student, Sera. And we will both continue to behave appropriately. Now get into position."

It was an order: he didn't even say please. Sera complied.

It felt like the longest session ever. Mr Marek was intent on his work, barely speaking to her, and it had gone from the best birthday ever to the worst. It was going to take a lot of drinks tonight to get the party spirit back.

He could have at least tried to be nice on her birthday. She watched the dark head, the strong hands. Looked at him frowning at her and back at his canvas, trying to get the details right. She sometimes guessed from the colours on his brush and palette what particular element he must be painting.

Given this was currently a rich crimson she assumed he was working on the drape behind her. She may as well not even be there. Surely he could have painted it without her?

So why did he want her there?

* * *

At the end of the session Mr Marek was still in a dark mood so Sera didn't dare repeat her request for a birthday kiss.

Inwardly she was crushed but determined not to show it.

As Mr Marek opened the front door to let her out, she saw a silver sports car parked right outside, with a blond man emerging from it. Sera wasn't an expert when it came to cars but it looked very sleek and expensive.

The man approached up the front path and instantly gave her the eye. He was tall, like Mr Marek, and good looking in a somewhat languid, dissipated way. He wore a flawlessly cut grey jacket.

"Hello. I hope I'm not interrupting anything?" His tone was lazily curious, with a suggestive innuendo behind it.

"You're not. She was just leaving." Mr Marek looked annoyed. He obviously knew the man but Sera couldn't tell whether he had been expecting him or not.

The blond man looked at him and then at Sera. "Don't tell me you're giving private art lessons, Tarq?" His eyes, heavy-lidded, skimmed up and down Sera, making her feel as exposed as if she had just slipped off her robe.

Yet he was undeniably attractive. Certainly Lois's type.

"I'm Sera." Trying not to let him realise that his brazen eyeing-up had had any effect on her, she held out her hand.

The blond man took it. His grasp was warm and firm. "Lionel. A very old friend of Tarquin's. And I suspect you're a deliciously new one?"

Sera almost laughed except she caught Mr Marek's gaze and saw that he was furious. His tone masked irritation when he spoke. "Lionel and I were at art college together, and he's shown some of my paintings in his gallery."

"Which is exactly why I'm here. To discuss your new collection, which I'm still waiting for."

"Which you can keep waiting for."

Lionel was unruffled by his friend's attitude. "I am endlessly patient. Why don't we all have a drink if you don't want to talk business?" He turned to Sera. "I've been trying to persuade our mutual friend" - he drew out "mutual friend" - "to actually pick up a brush and paint me something I can sell. Now I'm beginning to realise why he's holed away up here, distracted from his work."

He shot Sera a wickedly sexy grin and she blushed.

"You're holding up Sera, she needs to leave." There was now an icy edge to Mr Marek's voice.

"Am I? Surely you're not in that much of a hurry to get away, are you? It's not like Tarq to chase women away. Just one drink. Perhaps Sera can help persuade you where I've failed?"

Mr Marek glared at him. "A drink won't be possible, I have other things to attend to."

"You attend to them, and I'll attend to the lovely Sera." Lionel gave her another flirtatious grin.

The compliment and his shamelessly seductive tone made Sera blush. She was aware Lionel was just playing about, deliberately and very successfully managing to rile Mr Marek.

The art teacher tightened his jaw. "Go inside," he told his friend. "I'll be there in a minute."

His will was stronger and Lionel had to concede.

"Very well. At least I now know what the attraction is for you in this place." Lionel actually gave Sera a wink before going into inside the house and out of view.

Sera was about to go when Mr Marek spoke her name.

"Sera."

She stopped. Turned back to him.

"Happy birthday." He leant down and briefly brushed her lips with his.

It was like fire. Like ice. She felt a jolt in the pit of her stomach. Shock and instant desire.

But he turned abruptly and went back into the house, leaving her frozen to the spot and wondering what the hell had just happened.

14. Bonfire night

Black was the sky above, the bonfire burned their faces hot while their backs froze with cold. Sera was wearing gloves but her fingers still felt stiff. She watched the flames crackle and soar. It was an absolutely vast pyre.

"I love Bonfire Night," Lois was saying. "The frostier it is, the better the fireworks look."

They were high up on Romany Hill where a local farmer put on an annual pig roast and fireworks display. It was supposedly to commemorate Guy Fawkes and the Gunpowder Plot, but Sera always felt it was far more primaeval than that. Beacon fires lit against the oncoming winter: a last defiant show of human spirit before the ice and cold and darkness closed in.

It was one week since her birthday and as she had come to expect, Mr Marek was blowing cold again. They'd also had to skip today's session because he had to sort things out for his father.

Sera hadn't told her friends about the kiss. She wasn't sure exactly why; perhaps it felt more significant to keep it to herself, hugging her secret inside herself.

Also there wasn't much to tell. Nothing had happened since, and maybe it didn't mean anything. After all it had been kind of perfunctory. Maybe it was just politeness, given she had requested it.

Though he had chosen to kiss her on the lips not merely the cheek...

Joel and Lois had gone off on a quest for more food and drink, leaving Sera temporarily alone. As she stood holding a sparkler, and realising she didn't have a way to light it, she spotted Janette from school.

"Hey." They greeted one another. Janette was wearing a bobble hat and a thick scarf, the firelight reflected in her glasses.

"It's a great bonfire, isn't it?" Janette said.

"Bigger than last year."

Janette gazed at the flames. "I love fireworks and fires," she said. "They're so clear and bright and colourful."

Sera had never liked to ask Janette about her vision problems but now she felt bolder. "I noticed you use a lot of colour in class. Do you find certain colours easier to see?"

Janette was happy to answer. "Bright things, yes. They're much clearer."

"I wondered what exactly your eye condition was?" Sera asked.

"Multiple things, since I was a baby mainly. The good news is that I got cleared for a driving license, thanks to these - " she indicated her thick lenses " - though I choose not to drive at night because it's much harder."

Sera was impressed by her spirit. It couldn't have been easy for Janette growing up and going to school with hearing aids and huge spectacles. Children could be cruel. Janette had only joined their school in the sixth form and Sera hadn't got to know her very well.

"If you'd like a lift back, feel free. Lois drove and there's plenty of room."

Janette smiled. "Thanks, but I already have a lift. I appreciate the offer. I loved your picture of Lois in class the other day. Do you know what you're going to do for your main project yet?"

Sera didn't, and it was something that she was starting to stress about. So much rested on it, her exam results and probably her whole future. "Not yet."

"Me neither. Other than it's going to have to be a huge canvas with plenty of bright colour."

They chatted for a few more moments and then Janette left to rejoin the people she was with. Where were Joel and Lois? Sera wondered. Either one of them or both were doubtless getting chatted up by some hot guy. It surely couldn't take this long to queue for baked potatoes and mulled cider?

Sera still wanted to light her sparkler and Lois had the cigarette lighter. None of them smoked but they had brought it especially for this purpose. After all, what was Bonfire night without sparklers? Making glittery circles and tracing letters in the air.

Would it be safe to somehow stick it in the embers of the fire? She took a step closer and realised that her face would melt if she approached any nearer, so stepped back again. It really was a furnace.

As she looked down wishing she had a box of matches, a lit sparkler, fizzing its white fire, was pressed against the tip of hers. She looked up, expecting to see Joel or Lois, but it wasn't them.

Instead it was the last person she had expected to be there.

And the one she wanted to see most of all in the world.

Mr Marek.

Just as she looked up at him her sparkler finally flared into life, catching alight from his, and she started.

"Sera."

He looked Satanic in the firelight, the flames dancing over his face and the blackness of night behind him. He could so easily have avoided her, she was surprised he had actually come to greet her.

Let alone light her sparkler for her.

"Thank you for the light." She shivered, suddenly feeling the contrast of hot and cold again. When you turned from the fire the air was icy.

Without speaking Mr Marek took off his scarf and wound it around her. It was soft and light and warm.

"I can't have my muse getting frostbite." His expression was cynically amused, even in the darkness she could see the gleam in his eyes.

"Only frost bite?" Sera emphasised "frost".

"You had some other bite in mind?" His face was shadowed, his height loomed over her and Sera felt both turned on and momentarily scared.

"Maybe." She let her lips part slightly after she said this. *I'm here*, she thought. *I'm right in front of you and I'm warm, and it's freezing on this hill, and I know we both want this.*

84

Mr Marek wavered. He leant closer to her. "You are far, far too young for me," he said, his voice a seductive murmur.

Sera closed her eyes.

She felt his lips brush hers, so warm against the chill of the night air. Before the kiss could deepen he broke off. She opened her eyes, confused, but his hand brushed her hair back and roughly pulled the scarf aside.

For a second the icy air on her neck made her shiver and then the heat of his mouth covered her skin, making her gasp. He was sucking and drawing on her flesh as his teeth grazed her lightly.

It almost hurt but it was a good pain: she wanted more.

But he broke away from her once again.

"I can paint over a love bite." His smile was sardonic, there was triumph in his gaze. Doubtless at her shocked reaction, he must have heard her gasp.

Before she could react there was a voice to the side. "Sorry we took so long, the queue was forever." It was Lois. Sera turned to her, then back to Mr Marek.

He had gone. Vanished.

She tried looking for him among the crowd of people but it was so dark away from the fire that it was impossible to spot anyone.

"Who are you looking for?" Lois asked.

Sera looked at her sparkler, which had just died out. "Mr Marek was here."

"Was he? I didn't see him," Lois said.

Where had he disappeared to so quickly? Had she imagined the whole thing? Wondering, Sera touched her neck where he had embraced her. Then she felt the scarf. His scarf. So it was real. She had physical evidence that she wasn't delusional.

Joel handed her a cup of cider. "Are you sure you're not hallucinating? Heat from the fire making you swoon?"

"No, he gave me his scarf. See?" Sera showed him.

"He gave you his scarf? Why would he give you his scarf? It's cashmere, good quality too. Expensive. He has taste, anyway." Joel typically ended up more interested in the item of clothing than the question at hand.

"He said he didn't want me getting cold."

Joel was incredulous. "Marek came up, just gave you his scarf, and vanished?"

Not quite. "He lit my sparkler too."

Lois started laughing. "Sorry, Sera, but it sounds so bizarre. I mean showing up, lighting your sparkler and handing you a scarf. Like the imaginary bonfire fairy."

"And he kissed me."

That shut Lois up. "Seriously?" Joel asked.

"Only very briefly, like before." Damn. She hadn't meant that to slip out.

"What?!" Now both Joel and Lois were rounding on her, demanding answers. Sera was going to have to tell them everything.

Just then the sky cracked into a cascade of fiery colour. The fireworks had started. "Come on! Let's go nearer the lake, the reflection is amazing there!" Lois dragged Joel off and they disappeared into the crowd once again.

Sera never knew what made her linger, why she didn't go with them. The view was better on the other side. But she held back, alone once again.

As she stood there two strong arms slipped around her waist from behind. She felt herself pulled against a hard, strong body.

She didn't dare turn around. He was back. She closed her eyes for a few seconds, opening them at the next explosion of colour. It was warmer with him holding her, though her whole body felt shivery in a different way.

While the sky was lit up with golden showers and dazzling rockets and exploding chrysanthemums his lips were on her hair, brushing it aside, behind her ear, on her neck. She whimpered when he embraced a sensitive spot and hoped he didn't hear. It was very hard trying to just stand there. Sera knew her breathing was increasing.

She wanted to twist round and face him, have him kiss her properly. She longed for him.

But she sensed he was doing this deliberately. After all he hadn't tried turning her around. He was playing a game with her and so far, he was winning.

The fireworks reached their climax and died away but Sera was left on edge. She wanted them to go on forever, because as soon as they stopped, she knew he would withdraw.

"I'll see you in class." His voice, near her ear, was husky.

Sera swivelled around then and looked directly at him. Mr Marek ran a finger around her cheekbone and over her lips, tugging on her lower lip.

Please kiss me. It must be written all over her face.

But he simply smiled at her, a strange, inscrutable smile, and melted once more away into the darkness.

15. Fainting couch

It started with a tickle in her throat. That typical dry, scratchy feeling. Sera tried to ignore it. Lois had already called off their Saturday night plans due to a virus and Sera had a horrible feeling that she was coming down with the same.

But she absolutely couldn't miss her session with Mr Marek today. It was their fifth and final session and it felt like her last chance. After today she would never get any alone time with him again. She would be reduced to hoping to bump into him in a bar and getting him drunk or something.

There was the folk concert coming up but everyone would be there, and it hardly seemed like a sexy setting.

So it was now or never.

Sera had no idea what Mr Marek had been thinking on Bonfire Night because he had made no allusion to it during the week or in the evening class. He hadn't come for the usual drink at the Norfolk Arms either, claiming he had to see to his father which was probably true. His father hadn't been able to come straight home from hospital as planned due to a few complications with his knee, which he had injured when he fell.

Skipping breakfast as she felt queasy and had no appetite, Sera wrapped up warmly in the bitter November air and walked briskly across town. Her family were away at Marisa's parents' house. Once again Sera had used homework as an excuse though of course the real reason was her modelling session with her art teacher. Neither her father nor Marisa had guessed anything, thankfully. Sera had managed to create the impression that she and Lois had a regular study session on Saturday lunchtimes.

There was Catalina, still under her tarpaulin dusted with decaying leaves and twigs. Did the people who owned the boat ever take it out?

For the last time she quickly undressed in the study, donned the robe, went to the couch and lay in the usual position.

Mr Marek worked intently that day, not talking. He was near to completing, she assumed, and perhaps needed to concentrate.

Sera tried to remain still. She felt more and more tired and stiff and aching the longer she lay there. The heater didn't seem to be working properly. She felt cold. Very cold and shivery. But also hot. And tired. Momentarily she closed her eyes then realised she couldn't keep her teeth from chattering.

"Sera?" Mr Marek was looking at her, concerned. Not in the usual way he did to paint her. "Are you alright?"

"I'm fine." She could do this. She wasn't going to fall at the last hurdle.

"You're very pale. Are you sure you're okay?" He came over and felt her forehead. "Christ, you're burning up. Get your clothes back on immediately." He helped her put the robe around her but by then she was shivering uncontrollably. "You're clearly ill. I'll drive you home. Are your parents there?"

"They're away this weekend."

He swore again. "You shouldn't be alone."

The light was starting to do strange things in front of Sera's eyes. A weird grey fuzziness like the static on an untuned television was appearing around the edges of her vision. She was almost fascinated by it but she couldn't stop it.

It moved across, closing in, clouding everything out, and she found herself sinking to her knees. Everything was disappearing, her body ached so much.

"You need to lie down. Come here."

Half lifting her, half guiding her Mr Marek managed to get her up the stairs and into a bedroom. Still wrapped in the hotel robe, Sera was put into a bed and the covers pulled over her. It was soft but so cold, the sheets were chill.

"I'm so cold." Her voice was barely a whisper. She felt as though she were in a dream. Everything ached and she was so cold. So very cold. She was shivering violently.

He slipped into the bed behind her and wrapped his arms around her, trying to keep her warm. He was fully clothed but he was warm through the fabric. She needed heat. "Please don't leave me."

Then the world went black and Sera knew nothing else.

* * *

Sera was so warm and the pillow beneath her head was so soft.

And exhausted. She felt so tired and when she opened her eyes a chink the light hurt them and she closed them again. She tried to figure out what was happening. She wasn't in her own bed and she wasn't alone. A heavy arm was draped over her.

She felt a second of panic. Where was she?

Then vague memories came back to her. Oh God.

She was in bed with Mr Marek.

Were it not for feeling weak and exhausted she would have leapt out of bed in embarrassment. She couldn't even remember exactly how she had got here. The last thing she remembered was lying on his couch feeling terrible. What had happened?

"Sera?"

He must have sensed that she had woken. He didn't move though, he remained there holding her. Keeping her warm.

"I'm so sorry." It was all she could think of to say.

"It's not your fault you got sick. I feel worse that I kept you lying there not realising how ill you were. How do you feel now?"

"Okay." Which was a lie. Sera moved the top of the blanket and it sent some cooler air down. Suddenly she was freezing again, shivering. "Still cold."

"You've got a fever. You should take a hot shower. I'll fix it up for you."

He left her, huddled in a shivering bundle, and came back a minute later. "It's running. Take as long as you need. There are clean towels. And if you want me to call anyone, or a doctor, I'm happy to do so. I can drive you wherever you need."

In her feverish state Sera interpreted this as him wanting to be rid of her and felt bereft. After all, she had caused him enough trouble. Nonetheless she needed heat. Wrapping the robe around her - it seemed horribly thin and insubstantial now - she managed to stumble to the bathroom which was already warm with steam. She stepped inside the shower and stood there, letting the hot water drown her.

It felt so good.

It felt nearly as good as the heat of Mr Marek's body, holding her.

The water drummed down onto her for what seemed like ages, though it was probably only a few minutes. She was conscious of his hot water running out: was it on demand or coming from a tank? She hoped the former. Not so much for the sake of Mr Marek's water supply but because she wasn't entirely certain that she would ever be able to leave the shower. She felt that she was never going to be warm again and would need to stay in its heat for the rest of her life.

Soon enough however her body temperature rose and she was no longer shivering. Warm, then nicely hot. She put the robe back around her and stood there in the hot damp steam.

Sera knew from experience that it was a brief reprieve, once she cooled down the fever aches and chills would come raging back. But for moment she felt weak but comfortable.

She opened the door and returned to the bedroom across the landing. Mr Marek was there. He indicated a folded pair of pyjamas - his pyjamas! - and handed her a glass of water and two capsules.

"Cold and flu tablets, and put those on and get back into bed."

"I have to get home." She could see that the light was fading, it was nearly dusk. Given the time of year it would be dark soon.

"I'm not leaving you by yourself if there's the chance this could be flu. You can stay here and we'll see how you are later. Now get dressed."

Talk about a commanding bedside manner. Sera hurried into the pyjamas - thick, brushed cotton and many sizes too big for her - while Mr Marek turned his back to afford her some privacy. Kind of ironic given he had seen her naked many times.

"Thank you. They're very comfortable," she said, so he would know she was clothed again.

He turned back around, eyeing the pyjamas with some amusement in his gaze. "They were actually a gift from a well-meaning aunt. They're clean, I've never even worn them."

"They didn't fit?"

"I sleep naked."

Their eyes met with a brief flare of challenge in his. Sera swallowed. She took the glass of water and managed to take the pills. Looking around she realised that this must be the master bedroom, given its size and the fact that there were personal items in here, such as an alarm clock by the bed and a couple of books.

"Isn't this your bedroom?" she asked.

"If you're worrying that I'm going to take advantage of you while you're ill, you can set your mind at ease. I'll be sleeping in the spare room."

Damn.

"You stayed here before. I don't want to kick you out of your own bed." Sera desperately wanted to be wrapped up in his arms again but she could see that he was resolute.

"You rest now, and I'll check on you later." It was another command. Sera was exhausted and weak and aching. The pyjamas and the bed - Mr Marek had put an extra quilt on - were warm.

It wasn't hard to obey. She didn't dare do anything else.

16. Morning after

If Mr Marek had checked on her later Sera wasn't aware of it as she had slept straight through. It was already daylight when she awoke. She felt much better but had the weak, hollow sensation of having had a fever.

She could smell coffee and actually felt hungry which was a good sign, since she hadn't eaten anything the day before.

She was in his bed!

If only he were there too. Sera was half tempted to wait until Mr Marek came upstairs to see how she was and then try to lure him in between the sheets.

Then she remembered she probably looked terrible, with her hair a complete mess and no make-up. She slid out of bed, put the robe on and crept to the bathroom.

One hot shower later - why did men never use conditioner? - and after attempting to brush her teeth with her finger and some toothpaste, she decided it was time to go downstairs. She had no choice but to wear the robe as her clothes were still in the study.

"Are you feeling better? You still look very pale," he greeted her. He looked amazing himself, well refreshed, his hair thick and dark, offsetting the flawless angles of his face.

And those lips... the very ones that had briefly made contact with hers. Twice.

"Much better, thank you."

"Well enough for some coffee? Breakfast?"

Sera accepted a coffee. She figured she could probably eat a piece of toast.

"Just a piece of toast? Nothing on it?" He was spreading butter on his. Proper butter, not the horrible spreadable low-fat stuff that Marisa kept in the fridge. Sera and her father were always sneaking real butter in.

"Just toast is fine." She sipped the coffee he handed to her and wondered whether she could drink it without sugar. It was very black and strong.

As if guessing her thoughts he pushed a sugar bowl to her. "If you take sugar."

It was a very weird situation, Sera thought. The kind of awkward morning-after scene that you might experience if you had just slept with someone. Except she had spent the night in a separate bed with a fever. If only she hadn't been ill, maybe it would have been quite a different night.

Though it was only because she had been ill that she was here at all. She half-wished it was full blown flu so she could have stayed with him for the week.

"Sorry for everything yesterday, and for cutting the session short," she said.

Mr Marek poured another coffee. "You're hardly to blame. Besides it just means we'll have to have one more session." His eyes locked on hers as he said this and Sera felt her stomach flip with anticipation and joy. One more chance to be alone with him. She would definitely not squander it by being ill again.

The doorbell rang. Mr Marek frowned. It was still early on Sunday morning, not the sort of time that one usually got callers. Too early for Jehovah's Witnesses even.

Sera felt a cold finger of dread that it was her parents at the door. But they were a hundred miles away, and besides they had no idea of this address. She had refused even to tell Lois and Joel where Mr Marek lived, lest they try to come round and peek through the windows one Saturday. Sera wouldn't have put anything past Lois. Or Joel, for that matter. Neither of them would have been able to resist.

He went to open the door and Sera heard a woman's voice. "So this is where you've been hiding out, Tarquin? I finally managed to get an address from Lionel. I don't know what you were thinking, quitting London without even leaving a forwarding address."

"Victoria, it's a not a good time..."

"Since I've driven all this way, the least you could do is invite me in for a drink, darling."

Sera didn't hear his reply before a woman pushed her way into the room.

"And who might this be?" She looked extremely displeased to see Sera.

The woman was tall, with expensive but artificial looking frosted blonde hair, her face immaculately painted. She also looked quite a bit older than Mr Marek, in her late thirties at least. She was also very glamorous. Sera felt drab in comparison.

Mr Marek returned to the kitchen behind her.

"This is Sera. She models for me."

Victoria arched her pencilled eyebrows. "With wet hair? What is she, a mermaid for one your seascapes? Or is she living here?"

"Sera does not live here, and that's none of your concern," Mr Marek said. His face appeared calm but from the set of his jaw Sera could tell he was furious. She hoped it wasn't with her. If this Victoria was his girlfriend - and her heart sank at the thought - her presence there would doubtless be causing a lot of issues.

"I should be getting back anyway," Sera said, conscious that Victoria was clearly displeased by her presence. "I'll just go and change."

Sera slipped off to the study where her clothes were, trying to remember if she had left anything upstairs. She didn't think so. She could hear Victoria's voice as she went, it rang through the house.

"How very cosy, holed up here with some young girl. I should have thought you'd have more sense and discernment, Tarquin."

Sera tried not to eavesdrop but she couldn't help it.

"I'm here because of my father," Mr Marek was saying.

"How frightfully convenient to find a ready supply of models in town as well." There was an unpleasant ice in Victoria's tone.

"I don't see that it should concern you either way. What I do in my professional and personal life is no longer your concern."

No longer? Sera felt a pang of jealousy towards Victoria that it had at one time been her concern.

"Darling..." Syrup re-infused Victoria's voice. "I came here hoping we might discuss all that."

Mr Marek's curt reply suggested he wasn't responsive to her entreaty. "I suggest you go back to your husband, Victoria."

"That's why I'm here. I've left him."

There was silence after this, or at least Sera couldn't hear Mr Marek's reply, and she had the horrible fear that the two of them were suddenly locked in an embrace. But she really couldn't draw out putting her clothes on any longer. She wished she had some make-up with her so she wouldn't look at such a disadvantage against the sleek and painted Victoria.

Part of her wondered whether she should just slip out of the front door and make her way home. The situation was so hideously awkward.

Gathering her jacket she summoned her courage and went back into the kitchen. Victoria appraised her jeans and jersey with something of a sneer. Mr Marek wasn't there and Sera didn't like to ask where he was, though her face showed confusion.

"Tarquin is in the bathroom," Victoria told her with a tight-lipped smile. "I suggest you run along."

Sera was about to do just that when there was a voice in the doorway. "That won't be necessary. I'll drive you home, Sera."

Sera mumbled something about being happy to walk.

"It's not up for discussion. You've been ill." Mr Marek ignored Victoria's look of fury. "Let's go."

Feeling hostile eyes upon her back as they exited the house, Sera was relieved to get away. She could tell Mr Marek was furious so didn't dare try to make conversation. Despite trying to tell herself she didn't care and that it was none of her business, she was burning up with curiosity about Victoria and him.

They drove in silence until they reached Sera's house.

She thanked him as he opened the door for her. "I'm sorry I got ill." She meant that she was sorry for being in the way of his girlfriend or ex-girlfriend and causing tension, but she couldn't articulate it.

"It wasn't a problem." He glanced at her, and for a moment Sera wondered if she saw a flicker of tenderness in his eyes. Knowing what he was usually like, however, she suspected it was actually relief to be finally rid of her.

So he could return as soon as possible to the glamorous frosted blonde waiting for him back at his place. Sera felt heavy with misery at the thought.

"Anyway, thanks for everything." She wished there was a way she could return the favour. "For giving me your bed and looking after me, I mean."

Mr Marek paused, looking down at her. "If you hadn't been ill..." he began but left the sentence unfinished.

Sera looked at him questioningly. "If I hadn't been ill?"

"I might have been tempted to look after you in quite a different way."

Abruptly he left and returned to the car, leaving Sera standing there stunned. Did he mean what she thought he meant? What she hoped he meant? And what about Victoria?

17. Folk concert

As anticipated, Elizabeth was merrily singing about having a lovely time in Bangor as her folk band played their various instruments. There was a banjo, a violin and an accordion. It was all very lively but a world away from the kind of music that Sera usually listened to.

Everyone from the evening class was there - Bob having kindly given Sera a lift in his car - as well as Lois and Joel who had insisted on coming after Sera made the fatal error of mentioning the event to them.

"We'll have to be there. To see you and Marek looking fondly at one another over folk music, we can hardly miss that," Joel had said.

"You can't come. It will be way too awkward." If her schoolfriends came then there was no way that Mr Marek would make any further move, and Sera was still hoping he might kiss her again. A couple of beers, his inhibitions reduced...

She still didn't know what was going on with him and Victoria. Nothing had been mentioned at either school or the community centre. Sera hadn't even spoken to him alone since Sunday morning when he drove her home.

"You can't stop us," Lois said. "It's a public venue after all. We might have been dropping by The Green Man quite by chance. A nice country pub with a fireplace, on a wintry weekend."

"Except you wouldn't. We never go there," Sera reminded. They had all been there at one time or another, it was the kind of place you went for lunch with your family when relatives were visiting. But it was too far out in the country to be part of their regular weekend pub crawl.

In the end they had both shown up, Lois riding on the back of Joel's motorbike. Her curls always bounced back perfectly even after being crushed by a helmet. She gave Sera a breezy grin and joined the art group without waiting for an invitation.

If Mr Marek was surprised or bothered one way or the other he made no sign of it.

"These must be your artist friends," Lois said. "Are you going to introduce me?" Lois was a hit from the moment she flatteringly referred to everyone as "artists".

Sera, now squashed in between Lois and Winfred, was annoyed that she was even further away from Mr Marek. Joel ended up on the other side, soon lost in conversation with Jasper and Barry who seemed delighted by him. Sera could hear snatches of theatre conversation: Jasper was on top form with an audience as receptive as Joel, who loved musicals.

Lois seemed to really get into the folk music. "It's very cheerful, isn't it?" she said to Sera.

Sera supposed it was. Elizabeth had a lovely clear voice and the whole group were putting their hearts and souls into it.

"I wish I played an instrument," Lois said. "Do you play one, Sir?"

Sera wanted to die and sink through the floor when Lois used that term to address Mr Marek. She had so far managed to avoid revealing that he was also her school art teacher. But within seconds the secret was out.

"No wonder your work is coming along so well, Sera, getting all that extra tuition," Jasper said, a twinkle in his eye.

Sera desperately tried to change the subject. The last thing she wanted was for people to start remembering her impromptu nude modelling and the fact that she had also been Mr Marek's pupil at the time. Not that either of them had known, and that was a whole nightmare of complication in itself.

She was saved by the band taking a break and Elizabeth joining them. "Thank you all so much for coming," Elizabeth said, genuinely pleased by the support.

"It was a delightful performance, we all enjoyed it very much," Jasper said.

Conversation at once turned to the band and the songs and getting another round of drinks. Sera felt strangely detached from everyone else. As she sat there she looked up to see Mr Marek's eyes upon her. He seemed withdrawn as well.

At the end of the gig people made their various moves to get home. Lois gave Sera a knowing grin and sped off with Joel on his bike. Jasper and Barry also said their farewells. Eventually it was just Bob, Winifred, Sera and Mr Marek.

As Sera turned to go with Bob and Winifred, Mr Marek intervened. "I'll drive Sera home."

Bob protested. "It's no trouble at all."

"It will save you making two extra stops."

Bob looked at Sera to see what she preferred, unaware that Sera's heart had just leapt at the art teacher's suggestion. Keeping her face carefully neutral she simply said "that would be very kind" and the new arrangement was confirmed.

* * *

It was dark and icy cold in the carpark outside The Green Man. Sera was glad to get out of the chill wind even if the inside of Mr Marek's car was still cold.

She sat there, wondering what he wanted with her. He reached up and turned the interior light on.

"I have something for you."

He leant over to the back seat and brought across a large wrapped box, handing it to her. "Happy belated birthday. And thank you for all your time over the past weeks."

The package looked professionally gift wrapped and it was very heavy. Definitely not a bottle of wine.

"Can I open it?"

"It's yours, you can do as you like."

Sera was conflicted. She was desperate to know what was inside but she also felt awkward about tearing the paper off in a rough fashion like an over-eager child at a birthday party. Someone like Victoria would doubtless have carefully picked the bow undone

Sera did her best. She managed to tear off one corner and then gasped as she started to realise what it was. A set of oil paints, incredibly expensive, professional quality oil paints - she recognised the brand - and such a huge box! She extracted it from the rest of the wrapping and ribbons and opened the lid.

The top tray was suspended as a separate level, it was beautifully constructed. There were also accessories such as brushes and palette knives.

"I thought it was time you tried oils. You could even use them for your final A-level project," he suggested.

Sera, overwhelmed as she looked at the paints, realised she hadn't even thanked him. "I don't know what to say. Other than thank you of course, but you really didn't have to do this." She couldn't take her eyes off the colours: Alizarin Crimson, Burnt Umber, Ultramarine. Just the names were a poem, imagine what they could do on canvas.

"I want to see how you paint with oils," Mr Marek said simply.

Sera looked up at him. There were far cheaper ways for him to do that: he could simply have lent her some oil paints or even ordered some for school art class.

Normally she would have flung her arms around someone giving her a gift this amazing and hugged them, but she felt too constrained to do that with Mr Marek. After all he was her teacher, even if he had kissed her twice. And said all those things to her that still made her hot to think about.

"I hope I can do them credit," she said.

"You will. I have every confidence in your ability."

Sera currently had no idea what she was going to do for her final exam project. The themes were usually generic enough that you could do pretty much anything you wanted. She hadn't even figured out what medium she would use, but now she had these oil paints she knew it would have to be oils.

Which meant a lot of study and practice in using them. Caressing the tubes, she looked up at Mr Marek. "Will you teach me?"

There was a dark, sardonic gleam in his eyes. "What would you like me to teach you?"

Everything. For a moment they looked at one another, Sera felt spellbound. Here she was with him in his car, in the dark. She knew he was attracted to her. He knew she was attracted to him. The only thing stopping them were his scruples.

She didn't dare to utter what she would have most liked him to teach her. He could almost certainly guess. So she stuck to her original wish. "How to paint with oils."

"I'm sure we can schedule some classes on that."

Sera was a bit dejected by this response, she had hoped that he might suggest private tuition not regular school classes. Overall she was still shocked and elated by the gift. Because it meant that he must truly regard her as having some ability in art.

Also, sexual attraction was one thing, but did this gift mean he actually liked her? And if he did, would he ever make a proper move on her?

18. Taken

Sera had drifted into a daze, reclining in her usual pose, when Mr Marek put his paintbrush down.

"It's done."

"Done?" She was confused.

"My painting is complete."

Sera's heart sank a little. She had known this was probably the final session, but she was still sad that it meant the end of all her private times with him. Lying there gazing at him and constantly hoping that he would break his resolve.

She expected him to tell her she could get dressed but instead he came over to the couch. He ran his finger down the centre of her body, between her breasts, to her lower stomach.

Sera gasped in shock, her skin shivering at his touch. Her nipples, hopelessly uncontrollable, tautened.

"And now." He left the sentence unfinished.

"Now?"

Mr Marek smiled, a note of triumph in his eyes. "Now I have completed my painting of the sexy little virgin, I can finally fuck you."

The shock was obvious on Sera's face. His eyes narrowed.

"I've spent enough weeks holding back while I painted you, with you wanting exactly the same."

"But you said..."

He cut across. "What I am saying now, Sera, is that I'm finally going to take you. I'm fairly confident you'll have no objections."

Sera could probably have thought of a dozen but her whole body felt electrified by his single caress.

"Open your legs." It was a command, not a request.

Feeling almost hypnotised, Sera parted her thighs. She was torn between embarrassment at exposing such an intimate area to him and desire for him to touch her there.

Which he did. He ran his finger down, brushing over her clitoris and making her jump and throb. "It's a huge turn on when you obey me," he told her.

His finger swirled around her entrance: Sera could tell that she was already getting very wet for him.

Despite this she was nervous. She had never done this before, and although she wanted to, the reality was more confronting than she had anticipated.

She played for time. "Shouldn't we go to your room?"

But Mr Marek had other plans. "I'm going to fuck you for the first time right here, exactly where I painted you."

He moved his hand over her breast, his thumb caressing her nipple and squeezing it between his thumb and forefinger. Just enough to cause slight discomfort and she winced, yet she still wanted more.

She could smell the heat of him through his shirt, his masculine aroma mingling with the soap or deodorant he used. It was a clean, sexy, maleness.

Then his mouth was over her, hot and wet, sucking and tugging on her skin. She arched up against him. His other hand slid between her legs, flicking past her most sensitive place, dipping inside her. He put one finger up inside her, moving it around gently.

"Very tight and very wet. But I know you can take a little pain from me, Sera."

He switched to two fingers which didn't hurt but felt full and stretching against her sensitive inner walls. He moved them in and out in a slow rhythm and she found her hips rising to meet him.

With his other hand she heard him unzip himself and then he took her hand and put it on him. He was huge, hot and hard. Her hand wouldn't even fit around him.

There was no way this was going to work. Absolutely no way. "I can't... it won't..."

"You will."

He began kissing over her stomach, up her body, over her chest and the hollows of neck. Paying attention to both breasts. He kissed up her throat and over her chin, and finally - at last - his lips came down on hers. Firmly, fully, tenderly. He made her mouth open as his tongue explored her.

His fingers were still sliding inside her and it felt like her entire body was his to command. She had no desire to resist him. She wanted more of him, closer, on her, against her.

Mr Marek broke off and stood up. Quickly pulled his clothes off so he was as equally naked as she was. Sera drew in her breath. He was so strong, tall and muscular. His body had looked powerful enough under fabric but underneath he was even more impressive. Hard, beautifully sculpted muscles, a broad chest, narrowing to leaner hips.

And between those hips, the unavoidable maleness that he was going to possess her with.

He moved over her, supporting himself away from her body as bent down to kiss her again. She put her arms around his back, feeling the lean cords of his muscles, loving being finally able to touch him.

His hand was back where she most wanted it and she couldn't stop herself from moving against him, writhing to try and get the right pressure and angle.

He withdrew it and laughed softly. "Patience. I'm going to be inside you for when that happens."

Then she felt him at her entrance, the huge head pushing slightly against her. She tensed, suddenly nervous.

He murmured in her ear. "I know you are far too young for me but you are the most beautiful thing I have ever seen."

Distracted and turned on by his words Sera relaxed back slightly and just then he started to push inside her. It struck Sera that they weren't using any protection but at that moment she didn't care. She wanted the bare, skin-to-skin feel of him within her.

Her art teacher, making her body his. Completely forbidden and wrong but so wonderful. She briefly imagined what would happen if people found out, then blocked the thought from her mind. She wanted this. They were both adults. He might be the one in a position of power but she was more than willing to yield to his desire.

But he was too big. It was too tight, hurting her, and he saw her bite her lip as he moved to kiss her.

"Relax, little one. I'll be as gentle as I can."

He withdrew a little and then pushed back again slowly, forcing her body to stretch further around him, trying to accommodate his girth. Sera wanted him so badly but the size of him made her nervous.

Rocking closer into her bit by bit, he alternated between kissing her to muffle any cries and murmuring more words in her ear - how much he wanted her, how beautiful she was, how incredible she felt to him.

Sera felt totally in his control and it made it easier to abandon herself. He was guiding her through this, she only had to trust him. And she had wanted him for so long.

Finally he was fully inside her. Huge and hard and heavy. She felt a mixture of discomfort and nervousness and also a desire to have him even deeper and fuller within her. The latter won out and she found herself involuntarily moving her hips towards his, trying to grind against him.

He smiled, a slow, sexy smile. "Do you want me, Seraphina?"

His use of her full name made her throb. "Yes." It was barely a whisper.

Mr Marek began moving in and out - making love to her properly - or at least that was how it felt. Sera had expected him to screw her hard and fast given what he had said, but he was tender and the way he looked at her made her feel cherished.

She knew it was probably just his way of trying to be gentle and relax her, but she let herself imagine that he actually cared for her. He wanted her badly, she knew that. He must like her enough to want her to enjoy this too.

So she gloried in his caresses, in his kisses. In the feel of him inside her, now the sharper pain had faded to a dull, strangely sexy ache. In the way he thrust and then twisted at the end of each stroke, giving her more pressure just where she needed it. His body seemed to instinctively know what hers needed.

He was silent as he drove into her, possessing her. His eyes seared into hers and Sera felt absolutely his. The thrill of her teacher doing this to her added to the sensation.

It was so illicit.

She could only imagine what other people would think. If her school found out she would be expelled. It would be the talk of the town.

His chest was so hard and defined above her, Sera found herself clinging to him, pulling him closer.

He whispered in her ear. "You feel amazing. I hope this is as good for you because there's no way I can hold back." His voice was ragged with desire.

A tingle of fear and desire ran through her body, knowing that he wouldn't let her go until he was finished with her. Not that she wanted him to stop. Ever.

Sera felt his rhythm increase, getting faster and harder, inflaming her own arousal with it. Her legs felt like jelly, her stomach dissolved, her lower body was nothing but an aching fire of stimulated nerves needing release.

"Come with me, baby. Together with me. Let yourself go."

Sera couldn't stop herself crying out at Mr Marek's words. His mouth was on hers again, his hands on her breasts, his maleness hard inside her, his hips grinding against hers. She felt driven to the edge of something, as though there was a bright light just below, and then she was tipped over it.

"Now, little one. Come for me."

She moaned and spasmed and writhed, completely abandoning herself as he thrust his hardest, gripped her hips, pulled her hard onto him and against him to maximum depth as he also spasmed and came.

Then he collapsed on top of her, nearly crushing her with his weight, his skin hot and slick with sweat against hers.

He cradled her. She was dizzy, exhausted. There were words on her lips and in her heart that she dared not utter. She said them silently, in her head.

Mr Marek recovered slightly and raised his full weight off her, enabling her to breathe more easily. "You were incredible, Sera." He brushed her hair away from her face where it was clinging with damp. "And even more beautiful after you orgasmed. One day I will paint you like this."

But right then he held her and for Sera it was the most perfect place in the world that she had ever wanted to be. In Mr Marek's arms.

When she thought of all the times that he had seemed angry with her to the point of hating her, right now this felt like exactly the opposite.

19. Aftermath

They ended up in his bed. Mr Marek had wanted to go again within a few minutes of finishing, but he could see from the apprehension in Sera's eyes that it was probably too soon.

He brought her a glass of water then suggested they go upstairs. "Come and lie with me. You don't have to be anywhere, do you?"

If she did, she would have cancelled without a moment's hesitation. "No."

Sera felt even more nervous going into his bedroom even though she had already been there, when she was ill.

"I barely slept at all when you stayed here before," Mr Marek told her.

"Really?"

"The thought of you, in my bed, only yards away. It wasn't easy."

Sera's stomach flipped at the thought of him thinking of her that way. "So you wanted me then?"

"I've wanted you from the first moment I laid eyes on you."

The surprise showed on her face as she lay there facing him, her head on the pillow.

Mr Marek's lips twisted in a smile. "That was why I was so angry. You showed up, late, and I knew you were going to be a distraction."

"You don't normally get distracted by models?" Not that she had even been a model, of course. Though she kind of was now.

"Normally they could be a pair of boots or a chair. They're interesting human forms to translate to a canvas, not sexual objects."

Sera wriggled down under the sheets, feeling glad that she was an exception. "I wasn't an actual model. Maybe that was why?"

"It's because you're the sexiest damn thing I've ever seen. You look like an angel and you paint like an angel. And you make love like an angel."

Make love? Did he really just say that? Sera supposed it was merely a more polite turn of phrase than screwing. It still gave her a warm feeling to hear the words on his lips. "I didn't really know what I was doing, you know, with it being..."

"...your first time?" He finished the sentence for her. "I should have been more gentle on you but after months of nearly going out of my mind with wanting you, it was hard to go as slow as I did."

Sera had a thought. "Did you plan this?" Was this the real reason that he wanted to paint her, so he could seduce her?

"No, I didn't plan it. In fact I did everything I could to resist. I took a cold shower nearly every time after you left. I wanted to paint you because you're the first thing I've wanted to paint since..." he broke off. Sera remembered the seascape. "Since a very long time ago."

Sera remembered something. "We didn't use anything." She felt awkward saying it but it had to be mentioned.

"I know. I wanted it raw the first time with you, no barriers, which was hugely irresponsible of me. I'm no saint, Seraphina. But if anything happened I'd stand by you."

She felt a strange lurch at the vision this momentarily put in her mind. "It's okay, I'm on the pill." She had started taking birth control when things were looking serious with an ex the previous year, and although that hadn't worked out she had kept taking it because it made her cycles so much lighter. That didn't cover everything though.

He read her mind. "If you're worried about the other issues don't be, I'm clean. I had a medical six months ago and there hasn't been anyone since."

Sera remembered Victoria. She had suffered a horrid fear that the blonde woman had managed to get back into Mr Marek's bed that day. So she was very relieved to hear it hadn't happened. She supposed Mr Marek could be lying but his gaze was so sincere. She felt she could trust him.

She realised she had always felt that way, which was partly why she had agreed to pose for him. Whatever character flaws he may have - and right now Sera couldn't think of any - he was definitely a man of integrity.

His finger was idly circling her breast, teasing her nipple, making her tingle. "You'll have to still call me Mr Marek at school."

The import of this was so huge that Sera couldn't process it. She simply said: "So you don't want me to call you that outside school, any more?"

"Christ no."

"So when you say at school, you mean at evening classes, I shouldn't call you Mr Marek?"

"I mean when you're with me, Sera." He looked directly into her eyes. "This wasn't a one off. I have every intention of continuing to see you."

She loved how he simply stated it, not even asking her. He took it for granted that she would comply with what he wanted. Which she would, a thousand times over.

Wanting to reach up and run her fingers through his hair to push it back off his forehead but somehow not quite daring, Sera asked. "So what should I call you?"

"By my name."

"Tarq." She automatically shortened it as Lionel had. Somehow it suited him more. And also because Victoria had called him Tarquin and Sera didn't want to sound like that woman.

Mr Marek's - Tarq's - eyes gleamed. "That's a hell of a lot better than Mr Marek."

"Or would you prefer Sir...?" Sera felt bold enough to tease him. She remembered he had winced when Lois addressed him by this term in the pub.

"Not unless you want a caning."

Sera was taken aback. "Is that something you usually do?"

"It's not part of my usual repertoire. However if you plan on misbehaving and feel that some discipline is required, we can work something out." There was a glint of amusement and desire in his expression.

Sera shivered. It all felt very far, very fast, but she loved it. She didn't particularly want to be caned, it seemed very harsh and painful. Spanked, though...

He chuckled. "Does that turn you on? What else turns you on?"

Everything he did or said turned her on. She was insatiable for him.

"How about if I pin you down you and refuse you release you until you come for me?" Saying this he gripped her wrists and held her arms above her head, pressing his weight upon her. It had the desired effect, Sera squirmed underneath him.

"It will be a nightmare if anyone finds out," she said, suddenly worried.

"We'll be discreet. Right now though I want you again. I'll go very slowly and very gently, but I've got to have you, Seraphina."

He moved over her, bringing his mouth down on hers. Forcing her to open for him so that he could taste her and entwine his tongue with hers.

Meanwhile his hand slipped down over her stomach, between her legs. He ran his fingers along her slit where she was already sensitive and growing wet for him. Sera shuddered.

"I need you, Sera. Take me inside you."

He pushed against her, his length already rock hard and ready. Stretching her sensitive flesh around him, requiring her to accommodate him.

She was tender from before so it was a mixture of pain and pleasure, but the closeness of him was like a drug. She needed him to make her body his.

Sera moaned softly and Mr Marek raised his head. "Am I hurting you?"

"Not really."

There was concern in his eyes but also heat. "So I am. Do you want me to stop?" He pressed the flat of his thumb against her button, moving it in a firm, circular motion.

She jerked and gasped at the sensation. "Not that. That feels amazing."

"It's both or neither, Sera." He wanted to conquer her through her own body, make her willingly accept whatever he wanted to give her. He stopped the circular motion and also withdrew from her. A double loss: her body craved his touch.

Then he pressed and pushed into her again. His thumb felt amazing but she was sore elsewhere.

He could read the conflict on her face. She was desperately turned on but also a little scared. He murmured near her ear. "Let me take control, baby."

He already had control of her but she knew what he was asking. "Please." Please take control, please be gentle, please never stop.

With a sudden movement he thrust her legs apart with his knees and drove into her, hard, deep, full. He was still rubbing her: tugging at her skin, rolling his thumb over her, harder as he entered her, distracting her from the soreness.

But it still hurt and she cried out. He covered her mouth with his to muffle her, turning it into a deep and sensuous embrace. Then he moved his lips by her ear again. "I've never wanted anyone as much as I want you. You're perfect."

Sera didn't know if he was serious but his words both reassured and inflamed her. For Mr Marek to want her this badly was a huge turn on. Despite trying to keep her at arms' length for weeks he now wouldn't let her out of his bed.

Afterwards she lay there, her head resting on his arm, neither of them speaking for a while. They were both spent.

"Do you want to stay with me tonight?"

Sera's first instinct was yes, absolutely. Before she answered him she thought through the practicalities. It was Saturday night and she often stayed at Lois's, so her parents wouldn't be concerned if she rang them and told them she was staying out. At least if they assumed she was at Lois's house.

Besides, she was eighteen. She could technically do what she wanted.

"I would, but I don't have any stuff with me."

"Stuff?"

"You know - clothes, a toothbrush," Sera explained.

He trailed his fingers over her stomach. "You won't need any clothes while you're in bed with me. As for a toothbrush, you can use mine, or I can pick you up one later, with some takeaway."

"Takeaway?"

"I would cook for you, but there's nothing in the house. Just let me know what you'd like. Chinese, pizza, Indian?"

Sera couldn't even think about food. She was still overwhelmed by everything that had happened. "I don't even know if I'm hungry."

"You will be." Mr Marek leant up on one elbow, looking down at her. He traced the side of her face. "I've certainly worked up an appetite.

Sera felt a momentary fear that if she stayed with him he might want to have sex all night and she was sore and exhausted. Mr Marek saw the shadow of concern pass over her face and interpreted it correctly. "I just want you to stay so I can be with you," he told you. "I know you need to get some rest. Despite my earlier actions I do have some self-control."

She gave him a mischievous smile. "Do you?"

"I held out for over two months. That probably deserves a prize."

"When I've recovered, I'll give you that prize," she promised.

His eyes narrowed, the heat rising in them again. "I'll claim it."

20. The painting

The doorbell rang and there was a loud knocking. Mr Marek swore.

Sera had a cold feeling it was Victoria again. "Shouldn't you get it?"

It was around ten o'clock on Sunday morning and she was freshly showered, wrapped in a robe, having tea and toast that Mr Marek had made her. He had been as good as his word the previous night, treating her with nothing but tenderness. Wrapping his arms around her while he slept next to her, cradling her against him.

She felt cherished. She had been worried it was a one off but he really seemed to want her there, and to see her again. "Now you've got a toothbrush here, there won't be a problem next time," he had said.

Sera felt annoyed that their morning peace had been broken. They had woken together, showered together and fooled around. She gloried in every moment with him. The water cascading off his perfect body, his lips on hers as it ran down over them and between them.

She had rung Lois the previous evening and Lois had been only too happy to cover for her once she had got over her shock. "Don't worry," she had said as Sera thanked her. "You now owe me a blow by blow account - literally, if that's what you two have been getting up to - and I will be calling in that debt."

But how could Sera relate most of it? It felt too personal, too uncertain. She didn't want to jinx things by implying they were more established than they were. She knew Mr Marek - Tarq, she must remember to start thinking of him by his first name - wanted to see her again, but it wasn't like there was anything official.

And now here was Victoria, to doubtless cause all sorts of trouble.

Sera braced herself as Mr Marek went to the door.

To her surprise and relief it wasn't Victoria who followed him back into the room. It was Lionel, the rather sexy blond man she had met a few weeks back.

He broke into a broad smile when he saw her there. "Well, well. Just what I'd like to find in my living room on a lazy Sunday morning, wrapped in a robe. Or is this a new pose? 'Seductress with toast'."

Lionel was joking but Sera saw Mr Marek bristle. Something in her was delighted by his reaction, and it inspired her to provoke more of the same.

"Would you like some tea?" she offered, putting on a playful smile to try and wind up her art teacher.

"I'd like something considerably stronger than tea. As well as something considerably sweeter," Lionel said, giving Sera a wink. He went over to the drinks cabinet and brought out a decanter. "You'll join me?"

The invitation was directed at Mr Marek who declined. "Not at this hour. And nor should you."

Lionel raised a hand in a nonchalant gesture, then pushed back his dark blond hair. "Enough lectures. I've just driven God knows how many miles to get here, and I need a drink." He poured himself one, Sera wasn't sure what it was.

"Exactly how many miles?" Mr Marek was not smiling.

Lionel laughed. "You always see straight through everything, don't you, Tarq? If you must know I was vaguely in the neighbourhood. Business and pleasure. So I thought I'd drop by on my way back to London for a bit more business. I didn't expect to find pleasure as well," he said, giving Sera an outrageously suggestive grin.

"You'll find neither here."

The ice in Mr Marek's tone failed to deter Lionel. "Come now. I know you're painting again because I can smell the turps. Unless you've started drinking that in despair?" This won him a glare from the art teacher. "You must have finished something by now. Show me."

Mr Marek was silent for a moment, clearly weighting up his response. To Sera's surprise he suddenly conceded. "Okay. But it's a one-off."

He led Lionel through to the conservatory-studio, indicating for Sera to follow. She had never yet seen his painting of her, for various reasons. The main reason was that he had never offered and she had been too shy to ask, not knowing what the protocol was between artist and model. Some artists were reluctant for people to see incomplete works.

And once it had been completed, well... Sera shivered, reliving Mr Marek's approach to the couch. What with that and everything else, there hadn't been time to even think of viewing the painting.

Now her other hesitations flooded back. The biggest now was that it would be mortifying to see what she looked like naked, in his eyes. From her own experience of portraiture she knew how different the final result could be, compared to a photo or a mirror.

Unable to decline the viewing she followed the two men to the easel. It was covered, presumably to keep dust off while the oils took their slow time to dry.

Mr Marek unveiled it.

And there, lying before them naked, was Sera.

* * *

Sera was torn between admiration for his skill and wanting the ground to swallow her up.

If only it had been of someone else, then she could easily have praised it.

Instead, there she was, naked, with her breasts and nipples and everything exposed, on a huge canvas.

Get over it, she told herself. She sketched nude models every week, it should be no big deal.

But it wasn't the nudity that was the issue. It was the expression on her face. It was so raw. He had captured her nervousness as well as her arousal. She looked like a turned-on virgin, which she supposed she had been.

Please strike everyone in this room blind, she begged the universe. Or make the damn painting melt or burst into flames.

Yet it stood there, immobile, with the two men gazing at it and Sera stricken with self-consciousness.

Lionel drew in his breath. "Christ."

Sera looked at Mr Marek. She saw a brief flicker of doubt in his eyes. It was the doubt that struck every artist, no matter how confident or experienced they were, that someone simply wouldn't get their art. That it wasn't as good as they hoped. That they had failed.

"It's... breathtaking. It's by far the most spectacular thing you've ever painted. And unlike anything else you've done," Lionel added. He looked at Sera, taking her measure more seriously this time. "The first and last of its kind, I suspect."

"Not necessarily." Mr Marek had relaxed now. "There's no reason I can't paint Sera again, do a whole series."

Lionel looked from him to Sera, taking in her robe and wet hair. "Not with that same expression though, I'll bet."

Was it really that obvious? Sera felt her face flush. She thought Mr Marek would deny it or get angry at the innuendo, but he didn't.

"Possibly not. But a different expression might be even more powerful."

"By all means. At least you've broken the drought. Even if you go back to seascapes I can get buyers lined up. Rather than fall out of favour you've only increased your curiosity and rarity value, Tarq. But then you always did have the devil's own luck when it came to art." Lionel viewed the painting again and then ran his eyes up and down Sera. She knew he was being deliberately provocative. "And the devil's luck in more ways than one, apparently."

Now Mr Marek did look as though he wanted to hit Lionel but he kept his irritation in check.

"Anyway," Lionel continued. "I've got a mixed exhibition in the spring, some established artists and some newer names. I'd like to include this, ahead of a new Tarquin Marek exhibition in the summer. If you can produce a dozen or so works by then?"

Sera, realising Lionel probably wanted to talk more detailed business, excused herself to go and get dressed. Mr Marek had put her clothes through the laundry and they should be dry now.

They were. Lovely and warm from the tumble dryer as well. Sera hugged them as she took them upstairs. She dressed, enjoying the freshness of the clean garments. There wasn't much else to do as her hair was still damp and she doubted Mr Marek had a blow dryer; besides she preferred it to dry naturally as it always ended up softer and shinier that way.

She slipped downstairs and went into the kitchen to make another cup of tea. She could overhear their voices though she tried not to deliberately listen.

"I don't know why the hell you had to give Victoria this address," Mr Marek was saying.

"She didn't get it from me. If she said that, she was lying. I expect she forced it out of Biddy." Sera wondered who Biddy was. Hopefully not yet another glamorous ex-girlfriend.

"I sent her packing." Sera, continuing to eavesdrop, was pleased to hear this.

She heard Lionel laugh. "I'll bet that delighted her. Maurice finally threw her out, did she tell you?"

"She told me she'd left him."

"She would." There was silence for a few moments, then Sera heard Lionel ask. "So how old is she, this one? She looks very young." He was obviously looking at the painting again and Sera felt the embarrassment creep over her.

Mr Marek's reply was curt. "She's of age, and it's none of your business."

There was dry amusement in Lionel's voice when he spoke. "She's less than half the age of your ex, I can just imagine how delighted Victoria would be by that. If she found out. Less than half your age too, I'll wager."

"Quit stirring, Lionel."

"As your agent, friend and business partner, I'd hardly do that. I'm just giving you a warning. Victoria's determined to get her claws into you again."

"Just tell her to stay away," Mr Marek told him.

"As if anything I could say would influence her. I'm afraid you're on your own where that woman is concerned. Still, you clearly have ample compensations." From the way he said "ample" Sera could guess he was looking at the portrait again.

She stepped back into the conservatory, pretending to have heard nothing. "Would either of you like tea or coffee?"

Lionel, who had finished his whisky or whatever he had poured himself, declined. "I have to be back in the city around lunchtime." London was a couple of hours drive so he would need to leave soon. "But I'll be back again soon and we'll have dinner," he said to Sera. "All three of us," he added quickly, seeing a dark look flare on Mr Marek's face.

"Thanks, that would be nice," Sera said, not knowing what she was supposed to say.

"Your image will be the star of the show. Everyone will want to meet you," Lionel told her. Before Mr Marek could react, Lionel rapidly said his goodbyes, made his departure and sped off in his silver sports car.

There was silence for some time after he had gone. Then Mr Marek - Tarq - turned to her. "You got dressed."

"It's mid-morning."

There was heat in his gaze. "I liked having you lying around in a robe. Much easier access." He slipped his hand under her top and fondled her breast through her bra. Sera could feel her body instantly react to him. "I should have burnt your clothes so you were forced to stay here, naked." He was only partly joking.

"You'd have had to write me a note for school tomorrow."

"I wonder if they've had 'sexual exhaustion' as a medication condition before."

"Sexual exhaustion?" Sera looked at him, a question and an invitation in her eyes. She felt fully recovered from the previous night and far from exhausted.

"Come here." Once again he commanded her into his arms and Sera knew he was going to do his best to make that condition a reality.

21. Misbehaving

School the next week was weird. Sera felt a suppressed thrill of excitement thinking about what had happened with Mr Marek but was terrified he might change his mind and go cold again.

After all it was a huge risk.

She'd had to tell Lois and Joel of course. Both of them were initially stunned though Joel tried to claim he'd seen it coming for ages.

"You still weren't expecting it to happen now though," Lois said as they sat in a secluded corner of the school cafeteria. It was too cold to eat outside. "Maybe after school ends next year."

This was about seven months away. Seven months of having to be extremely careful and discreet.

"So what's his body like?" Lois asked.

"How big is he?" This was from Joel, who was eating a sausage roll at the time and waggled it in a suggestive manner, making them giggle.

"Did he make any weird sexual demands?"

"Use turps as lube?"

Lois and Joel were making a joke of it partly to hide the fact that they were still pretty shocked by Sera's revelation. Some other students walked past them and took a nearby table, which restricted conversation.

"Just please act normally in class. Don't nudge me and give me really obvious looks all the time," Sera begged them.

Lois and Joel promised faithfully that they wouldn't. Sera didn't trust either of them but it would have to do.

"Is oil paint actually toxic?" Lois asked, licking yoghurt from the underside of a lid. "If you smeared it all over your body, would you die or anything?"

"We didn't smear any oil paint anywhere," Sera told her.

"I know that. I was just wondering. If you wanted to paint your skin, whether it would be safe or not."

"You need proper body paint for that," Joel told her. "Oil paint wouldn't dry, it would just run and smudge everywhere."

Lois looked thoughtful. "I was thinking of doing some busking in a costume. Like a living statue. Maybe paint my face gold or something."

Sera was intrigued. "You mean just stand there with a hat for people to put coins it? You'd have to look pretty spectacular. Would it be for charity?"

"For the Lois Christmas Bonus Collection Fund. I'm so broke. We can't all get paid to take our clothes of for sexy artists. Or have people stuffing fivers down our jeans," she added, directing this at Joel.

Joel grinned. He had recently had got a weekend job bartending at Orion and was rolling in tips due to his clean cut good looks and a very tight pair of Levis. "It goes in a beer glass not down my jeans. Though I mightn't mind if it did, if the customer was fit enough."

"Have you even been offered cash to go back with one of them?" Lois asked.

"Nearly every night. It's too risky though and my mum would kill me if she found out."

"Not as much as Sera's parents would kill her if they found out she was sleeping with her teacher."

This didn't help Sera's already jittery mood. "They'd go ballistic."

"When you tell them, let us know so we can come and hide under the window and listen in," Lois said.

Sera had no intention of ever telling her parents. There might be nothing to tell anyway if Mr Marek got cold feet.

"There he is now," Joel said. Sera felt her heart clench as she saw him across the dining hall. He was talking to the Geography teacher who clearly wasn't immune to his charms, tossing her hair as she spoke to him. It gave Sera a sharp pang of jealousy and insecurity.

122

"Miss Burrows is clearly taken with him," Lois said, stating the obvious.

It would be so much easier for him to date a colleague of his own age, Sera thought. It didn't help that Miss Burrows had ash blonde hair like Victoria. What if blondes were his thing?

"You've got nothing to worry about," Joel said, finishing his lunch and standing up to leave. "His body language is all wrong. He's not leaning towards her and he looks pretty indifferent to what she's saying. Whereas when he looks at you in class, it's like he wants to throw you over the desk and rip your clothes off. Which I suppose is pretty much what he's succeeded in doing, isn't it?"

* * *

"See if you can find the retarder, Sera. There should be some in the store room."

Sera was sent into the art room storage area, which was more like a large walk-in cupboard with shelves on three sides. Mr Marek was getting them to use acrylics that week, but the paints needed to be mixed with a substance that retarded their drying.

There were years of old supplies stacked up in the store room. Sera loved the smell of the art materials in there but the jumble and disorganisation made her heart sink. How on earth would she locate the retarder? She wasn't even sure what it looked like.

As she rummaged through a box of old brushes and paint tubes, she was roughly pulled around and pushed back against the shelf, with a hard thigh rammed between her legs.

She gasped. "There are people right outside."

The interior of the cupboard was out of view of the classroom but anyone could hear.

Mr Marek's eyes glinted evilly. He leant closer to her. "Come round to mine straight after school. And don't worry about changing."

"You mean just wear this?" Sera whispered, indicating her school uniform.

"Exactly that." He cupped her rear through her school skirt. "If I'm going to burn in hell, I may as well merit the hottest flames."

Then he left swiftly, carrying a pile of painting boards leaving Sera dazed and longing for him.

She could barely concentrate on anything for the rest of the day. She hadn't expected to have any interaction with Mr Marek until the Thursday evening class, when she had hoped he might offer her a lift home. And then drive her to his place...

Giving her a lift home from school would have been way too risky. Mr Marek didn't teach any classes in the final period that day so he was able to leave before her. Sera had to sit through French, which she was hopeless at on a good day, watching the clock tick down. She could have sworn the second hand was moving more slowly than usual.

As she walked to his place she was paranoid that someone would see her and wonder why she was going that way. What if another teacher drove past?

But no one else went that route and she arrived at number twenty-seven unobserved. Safe, for now.

* * *

The moment Mr Marek let Sera in the door he had his arms around her, pushing her up against the wall. Once again he pushed his leg up between hers.

"I nearly fucked you then and there in the art room. You have no idea what self-control it took not to dismiss the class and just take you."

Sera squirmed against the hardness of his thigh pressing against her.

"You like that, don't you?" he said. He pushed harder, pressing her against the wall and she whimpered. He had complete control over her body's responses, she was hopeless in resisting him.

He unzipped himself and sprang out huge and hard. They were still in his hallway, Sera hadn't even put her schoolbag down.

She let it drop as he forced her knee up, moved her underwear aside and thrust up straight inside her.

It was a strange sensation: he had to pin her to the wall with his body to stay inside her, practically lifting her off the floor, but it was close, deep contact. She wrapped her leg around him to make it easier.

He couldn't make big movements in that position so after a few moments he scooped her up, managing to stay inside her, and took her to the sofa where he crushed her body down on the cushions beneath his.

It was raw and ragged. He was caressing and moulding her breasts through her school blouse, her skirt was rucked up around her middle, she still had her shoes on.

Sera buried her lips in his neck, tasting his skin. Hot and damp with exertion. Her fingers clawed his back - he still had most of his clothes on but she managed to get under his shirt, loosening it so she could get access to his body.

Then he slipped his hand down and his thumb was again pressing firmly against her, making her moan and start to lose control. "I want to feel you come around me," he ordered her.

It wasn't going to take much, with him manipulating her body like that. Sera arched her back and felt her legs start to dissolve.

"Look at me Sera. I want to see your face when you come."

She wanted to close her eyes and let go but his eyes were fixed on hers. When she started to close them he commanded: "look at me" so she had to obey. Her body obeyed for her.

She looked up at him, his features dark and intense, a determination in his expression.

He increased the pressure. His eyes narrowed in a mix of lust and impatience.

Sera gasped and melted. She felt completely vulnerable and exposed: he could read every emotion and sensation on her face.

It overtook her. Her hips rose to meet him, matching his rhythm and the climax flooded over her in dizzying waves.

As it started to ebb he reached his own peak, hammering rock hard into her, turning her insides liquid.

"You are so damn beautiful," he told her. He drew out the words with each stroke.

He collapsed on top of her, hot and heavy, both of them perspiring and breathless. He was still inside her.

Eventually he rolled off and they lay there together.

After he had recovered for a few moments he spoke. "I'm going to need to fuck you in the art room. We'll make it work," he said quickly, feeling her startled reaction.

"But I have to have you there, at school, right where I teach you. Because right now all I'm doing every single art lesson is imagining it, and it's driving me out of my damn mind."

22. A threat

They lay together on the sofa for some time. Sera gazed up at the seascape on the wall. She found it both beautiful and disturbing. Haunting.

"Why didn't you paint for over four years?" she asked him.

Mr Marek didn't respond but neither did he grow tense at the question.

"Was it because of your mother?"

He turned his head to look at her, as though he were weighing up what answer to give.

Sera studied the planes of his face. The answer was in his eyes. "I do understand, you know. I lost mine as well."

Mr Marek frowned. "But you spoke of your parents?"

"I call them that. I guess they are, legally. But Marisa is actually my stepmother."

There was concern and sympathy in his eyes now. "How old were you?"

"Eight."

He lay back, looking up at the ceiling. After a long while he spoke. "My mother raised me alone for most of my childhood, it was just the two of us. My father was a political prisoner. She had no support, nothing. Her whole life was trying to keep a roof over our heads while campaigning for my father's release. Then there was the revolution and he got out and things were okay. But watching her get sick, die, not being able to do anything..."

He broke off and Sera felt his pain and remembered her own. Carrying the absence with her, no matter how long ago and how much she tried to bury it, it was always there.

She didn't need to say "I'm sorry" or commiserate, they simply understood one another. It was like being a member of the worst club in the world. A girl at school who had lost her mother in a car accident had once said this to Sera. Sera had resented it at the time and avoided her. She wanted her grief for herself. Then the girl moved schools and later Sera regretted shutting her out.

She wondered where the girl was now, if she had had a happy life. Sera's own had been reasonably happy even if she hadn't seen eye to eye with Marisa. Marisa had at least always been fair and tried to be kind. I should make more effort, Sera thought.

"I painted that while she was dying." His voice broke into her reverie. "You asked if it was a self-portrait. Now you know."

She sensed his mood change. He moved back over her, his lips on hers, moving down to her neck. "Being with you blots it out."

Mr Marek started to unbutton her blouse, kissing her stomach as he did so. He was much more tender than he had been before. He was just moving over her breast when the doorbell rang.

"Christ. I know no one in this town, are we always going to be disturbed?" He ignored it and returned to Sera who found it impossible to relax as the bell was pressed again after a few seconds. On and on.

"They must know you're in, your car's outside," she said.

Mr Marek looked exasperated. "Stay there, I'll get rid of them," he ordered her and went to get the door.

Sera reclined on the cushions, her clothes half undone, waiting for him to come back. She hoped he wouldn't be long.

Then she heard him address the visitor.

"What the hell are you doing here? Now is not a good time."

Sera couldn't initially hear what the visitor replied but she knew instantly that it was Victoria. Their voices became raised.

"Just go, will you."

"How dare you try to turn me away!"

"Victoria!" Sera heard Mr Marek exclaim and then realised Victoria had managed to force her way into the house. She sat up just as the blonde woman stormed into the room. She stopped dead in her tracks when she saw Sera. Mr Marek, behind her, closed his eyes.

Victoria spun around to him. "A schoolgirl, Tarquin. Are you serious?"

There was no way they could pretend Sera was just visiting, her dishevelled and unbuttoned school uniform more than gave the game away.

"It's none of your business. I'd like you to leave." A muscle clenched in his jaw.

Victoria did not leave. She was silent for a few moments, calculating. "She's not just any student, is she? She's your student. From the school you teach at."

"As I said, it's not your concern."

Victoria laughed softly, an unpleasantly menacing laugh. "Oh, but I think it's very much my concern, Tarquin darling. I wonder what the school would say? How these girl's parents might react if they were to find out?"

"Are you threatening me?" There was an even more dangerous note in Mr Marek's voice.

"I'd only be doing my duty as a concerned person to report something like this." Her smile was pure spite. Sera was starting to feel worried.

Mr Marek dismissed Victoria's words. "Sera is eighteen. No law has been broken."

"Nonetheless, I'm sure they have rules against fraternising. And how would it look? Painting your pupils - naked, I assume - and then seducing them. I can just see the newspaper headlines."

So could Sera. What would it take to make this awful woman go away?

"What is it you want, Victoria?" He sounded both irritated and resigned.

She laughed again, an artificial hollow laugh. "Why you of course, darling. Haven't I always wanted you?" Her gaze fell on Sera and her eyes narrowed. "And this little brat gone." She had nearly said another word beginning with "b" but managed to check herself.

"Neither of those things is going to happen."

"Isn't it? Let me be frank with you, Tarquin. I need a place to stay and I'm sure you have room here. If you get rid of that girl for good, I'm sure I can keep my mouth shut. Otherwise..."

Sera couldn't keep quiet any more. "You have no proof."

Victoria raised an artificially pencilled eyebrow. "Don't I? I should think the testimony of Tarquin's concerned fiancée, devastated to have caught him *in flagrante* with a school pupil, would be amply convincing."

Then she pulled out her trump card. Before Mr Marek could stop her she strode into the conservatory and pulled the cloth off the easel.

"And then there's this. More than sufficient evidence that very untoward relations have developed between you and your student. I must say, Tarquin, it's not your usual style. You'd be wiser to stick to seascapes now I'm here."

* * *

Sera was still reeling from everything Victoria had threatened, and she was even more alarmed to see Mr Marek looking conflicted.

Surely he couldn't be thinking of taking that awful woman Victoria back? Sera felt cold at the thought.

He rubbed his eyes. Victoria was hovering the doorway, awaiting a response.

"Please go into the kitchen. I need to talk to Sera in private."

Victoria hesitated for a moment, clearly reluctant to leave the two of them alone. In the end she did as requested but not without a sinister look of triumph on her face.

Never more had Sera wanted to slap someone.

When she had gone Mr Marek spoke to her in a lowered voice. "I'm not worried about me, Sera, they can all go to hell. I'm worried about the implications for you."

"I don't care either." Sera was determined to be bold.

"I'd get sacked, I know that. It's no big deal, thanks to you I'm painting again. But what would happen to you, would you be expelled?"

Sera thought about it. "Pretty much, yes." A girl had been exposed for dating her music teacher a couple of years previously and they had both had to leave in disgrace. If Sera was expelled she probably wouldn't be able to sit her A-levels but right now she

130

didn't care about that. She could always defer a year and go to a crammer. She told Mr Marek this.

"The last thing I want is for you to have to do that. And what about your parents? How would your family react?"

That was the real rub. If her father and Marisa found out she was screwing her art teacher there was no way they would support her studying art in London next year. She might try to work and save up and pay for it all by herself but it wouldn't be easy. "They'd freak out but I'd manage." The vision of Victoria seemed to make St Martin's fade further away. First delaying her A-levels and then university.

She couldn't lose him now. The thought of it made her realise how deep her feelings had grown for him. Not that she had any idea of his or how she stood with him.

"It's not just your parents," Mr Marek continued. "I know what she's capable of and the kind of salacious interest there would be in this. If the press picked up on the scandal it could be lethal for your prospects, Sera. Victoria has all sorts of connections in the art world. I don't want you branded as... in the way that you might be branded if it all leaked out."

He took her hands, trying to make her understand.

"For me it's different. A scandal wouldn't affect me nearly so much. I hardly had the reputation of an angel before. But I'm not about to disrupt your education, your relationship with your family, your entire life."

"You would rather have her come and stay here?" Sera couldn't believe she was hearing this. Victoria, in the very bed she had slept in. Gloating over her victory.

"I would rather the sun froze over. But I'm not wrecking your life."

Sera knew instinctively that there was no way she was going to change his mind. To convince him that she didn't care about school, only him. But how could she even say that to him? It wasn't like he had said that to her.

He tried to console her, while she felt the sun had already frozen over. "It's just for a few months. Hopefully she'll get bored sooner, but if not it's only until June. After that I'm out of here, it's a non-story."

Out of here... Sera's heart sank even further. She could barely speak but tried to keep her voice steady. "You're leaving in June?"

"My contract ends then. I'll still want to see you, though."

Hope flickered. "In June?" That far away?

"I need you like a drug, Sera. The addiction isn't going to go away." Mr Marek pushed a strand of hair off her face, tilting it up towards him. But he didn't kiss her, even though she longed for him to.

They gazed into one another's eyes, Sera feeling utterly hopeless.

"I won't be sleeping with her. I won't even be in the same room as her, whatever she tries. I'll get a lock." He was trying to make light of it but Sera felt as though she were plummeting downwards.

"If this is what you want."

"It's not what I want, baby." His voice was tender. "I just want to keep you safe."

23. The campaign

"The blackmailing bitch! How dare she?"

Both Lois and Joel were outraged on Sera's behalf when they heard about Victoria's threats and interference. The three of them had skipped school assembly for a crisis summit.

"I can't believe he'd give in like that," Lois said.

Joel disagreed. "I can. There's so much at stake, for the cost of what? A few months of waiting it out. A story like this would be murder. If the newspapers managed to get hold of a copy of that painting it would be splashed all over the place. Front page of the Sun. 'Dirty Dauber's Schoolgirl Scandal'. And the Daily Mail, you can just imagine them printing photos of St Christopher's and how much the school fees are."

"I almost want that to happen," Lois said. "If it was someone other than you I mean," she added quickly to Sera.

"'Pervy Painter's Sexy Strokes'. They'd have a field day. You'd have to leave town, they'd be camping outside your house. Sex is so much juicier than drugs when they want to do an 'exclusive private school pupils' exposé."

Sera thought Joel was seriously exaggerating but she genuinely feared what the tabloids might make of it.

"So the question is what are you going to do?" Lois asked.

"Do?" Sera hadn't even considered there was anything she could do. Except live in misery and anxiety that Mr Marek would have lost interest in her by June.

"To get the better of that bitch. You can't take this lying down, even if he's being all cautious or noble or whatever."

Sera looked from Lois to Joel. "She's right. You have to do something."

But what? How could Sera get something on Victoria that would give her the upper hand? She knew nothing about Victoria.

Though Lionel might. "I'll try Lionel. Maybe he can help."

Lois frowned. "Who's Lionel?"

Sera hadn't mentioned the gallery owner to the others. "He owns an art gallery in London. He visited the house while I was there. I don't think he likes Victoria."

"I suppose it's worth a try. What's he like, this Lionel?"

"Very dashing and flirtatious, but not in a serious way. The opposite of Tarq - Mr Marek - really."

After starting to get used to thinking of him by his first name, Sera now had to revert to Mr Marek. Anything else was unsafe.

* * *

Victoria had laid down her conditions - or rules, as they felt to Sera - for not reporting her affair with her art teacher.

Sera was to have no contact with Mr Marek outside class. No socialising, no more modelling, nothing. If Victoria suspected even the merest fraternising between them she would go straight to Sera's school and her parents.

So once again relations became distant and coolly professional in class. Sera was dying to be with him, to be able to linger after class and speak to him, but Mr Marek made sure that nothing happened.

She knew he was protecting her but still, it hurt.

At evening classes the cooler relations between them were noticed by other students. Sera saw Jasper giving her a quizzical look once or twice when the art teacher's manner was unusually brusque towards her. In fact Mr Marek had fought for Sera to remain in the class: Victoria had wanted her to quit, she claimed that unlike school, Sera wasn't required to be there.

It was the only point he won, arguing that it was part of Sera's education and he wasn't going to allow it to be disrupted.

In retaliation, Victoria started driving him to the class and picking him up afterwards. Once she even attended, keeping a beady eye on proceedings and leaving everyone else mystified as to

134

why their teacher's girlfriend was suddenly hanging around. The atmosphere was uncomfortable: no one really warmed to Victoria.

"Back on the scene, eh?" Surprisingly it was Barry who first commented on the situation to Sera. They were in the Norfolk Arms after class; Mr Marek was no longer permitted to attend.

"They've been together a long time, I believe." Sera hated being complicit in a lie but it was one of Victoria's conditions. Officially she and Mr Marek were a couple again. She had told him that once they got used to this again, their old affection would return. The thought turned Sera's stomach.

"I did think..." Jasper began, then stopped himself. "Well, there's no accounting for taste."

"A very odd woman," Elizabeth noted.

Sera was mildly comforted by this. She longed to tell them what was going on but she didn't dare. She agonised over what they might be thinking: possibly that Sera had had a crush on the teacher and been rejected. Or that they had had a brief fling and she had been dumped when his girlfriend returned. It was humiliating.

There was only one more class before the Christmas holiday. Everyone had signed up again for the Spring term which she was glad about. She would have missed them otherwise.

* * *

"Sera darling! I haven't been able to get the image of you out of my mind - clad or unclad. How's Tarq? Is he treating you well?"

Sera felt a momentary surge of joy at Lionel's acknowledging them as a couple.

"We're not really... it's complicated."

There were a couple of moments silence. "Something's up, isn't it? Tell Uncle Lionel everything. If I can help, I will."

Sera took a deep breath. "Victoria is back."

"Is she?" Lionel sounded puzzled. Sera filled him in.

Lionel's string of expletives sounded oddly elegant in his well-spoken voice. "I'll fix this, don't worry darling. Leave it to me."

It was a relief to have someone else that she could tell, someone on her side, but Sera felt bad for dragging him into it. "I didn't want to make it worse by telling you."

"You did absolutely the right thing. If that viper is coiled around his neck he won't be painting, and that's a problem for me. I never imagined she'd get this desperate. Maurice must have really put the screws on."

Sera thanked him. "If you can work some kind of miracle I'd be so grateful. I wasn't sure who else to turn to." The stress of it all was weighing her down. She lived in a constant state of fear that Victoria would tell anyway, out of spite. Or if she mistakenly thought that Sera was breaking her rules.

Sera was endlessly expecting a summons to the headmaster's office as well as jumping every time the phone rang at home. She tried to answer it as often as possible so if it was Victoria she could hang up. This strange behaviour had led her father and Marisa to assume she had some secret new boyfriend.

"In the meantime, why don't you come up and visit me in London? We'll have lunch," Lionel suggested. "There's no prohibition on you seeing me, I take it? Not that that vile hag would know one way or the other."

Sera didn't reply immediately and Lionel picked up on her hesitation. "Don't worry, I have absolutely no nefarious intentions. I've seen how Tarq looks at you. If I so much as laid a finger on you I'd lose not only all his business but also my life. I'd simply enjoy catching up. Bring a friend with you, if you like."

Given it would be the holidays the following week and she would have time on her hands, Sera agreed. It would be a good chance to do some Christmas shopping anyway. Lois was always up for a trip to London. And who could turn down a free lunch?

And did Mr Marek really look at her in a certain way? Right now she was grasping onto any crumb of hope.

24. Busking

Despite standing out in the street dressed up as a golden festive Tinman for several hours, the Lois Christmas Bonus Collection Fund was far from overflowing.

"You need to do something more dramatic," Joel said. "Like stand on one leg in an arabesque."

Lois pointed out that she couldn't hold such a pose for ten seconds let alone a few hours. She sipped her hot chocolate, trying to defrost. Sera and Joel had stopped by with hot drinks to give her some moral support.

"Oi! Yer not supposed to move!" a nasty little boy yelled at Lois. He had been pestering her for the past half hour.

"Fuck off."

"I'll tell my mum on you. And I wants my money back."

"You didn't put any money in, you horrible little brat," Lois told him. "Get lost or I'll tell that policeman you were trying to nick my stuff." There was some truth to this as the boy had been considering how he could grab some coins from Lois's hat when she was back in her statue pose. He fled.

"How much have you made?" Sera asked her.

Lois sifted through the donations so far. "About fifteen quid. A tenner of which was from an old gent who thanked me for not making any noise." Further down the street two young girls were performing dying-cat-torture on violins.

It was a typical Christmas scene: crowds of people in thick winter clothes milling about, laden with shopping bags full of presents that their relatives would probably return in the Boxing Day sales. The air was icy and the Christmas lights twinkled cold, garish colours up above them. Sera wondered what Christmas would be like in a hot country, Australia maybe. Did they bother with presents and carols and turkey or just hang out on the beach?

Just then Lois nudged her. "Over there! Is that her?"

It was Mr Marek with Victoria hanging off his arm. She was wearing a long camel coat with huge padded shoulders and looked very possessive of him.

Sera's stomach flipped and sank at the sight of them both. "That's her."

Mr Marek saw the three of them and raised his eyebrows in greeting. Before he could come over, Victoria pulled him in the other direction with a look of thunder on her face.

Sera felt quite bereft. She missed him so much. As he walked away from them he turned around and looked over his shoulder, catching her eye. Only to be forced to turn back around again by a violent tug from Victoria and some angry words that they couldn't hear.

They watched the couple disappear down the street.

"She is a bit glamorous, isn't she? All that hair and make-up just for a trip to the shops," Lois said. "The High Street is hardly Knightsbridge."

Joel was dismissive. "I prefer my drag-queens with a little less vagina."

Lois cracked up laughing but Sera wasn't in the mood to smile. "She doesn't really look like a drag-queen, does she?" Sera asked.

"Not really. You need actual class and style for that."

"She is beautiful though," Sera had to admit, miserable at the thought.

Joel shrugged. "For her age maybe. I bet she's had work done."

"How old do you reckon Victoria is?" Lois asked.

"At least a few years older than him. Maybe nearly forty?" Sera said.

This was met with a howl of derision from Joel. "Nearly forty? Are you both blind? That dame is nearer fifty than forty."

"You barely saw her, and only from a distance," Lois pointed out.

But Joel was adamant. "Trust me. It's obvious."

It wasn't obvious to Sera but she was mildly comforted by the thought.

* * *

It was fortunate that Lionel insisted on paying for lunch because Lois's busking money had been wiped out by the train ticket to London. Sera had offered to pay her fare but Lois refused. "I fancied a trip to Oxford St anyway so you don't have to pay for me."

It didn't help that they were going up on a Friday, which cost a fortune on British Rail even with a Young Person's Rail Card.

Sera had expected Lionel to be even more outrageously flirtatious with Lois than he had been with her but weirdly he wasn't. He still poured on the charm with Sera and did his best to lift her spirits.

"I'm afraid I've failed with Plan A," he told them. "I had hoped to convince Maurice to take her back. She desires her credit cards even more than Tarq. But Maurice has finally decided to put common sense ahead of sentiment."

"What's he like?" Sera asked.

"A very astute businessman and art connoisseur. And happily for me, an immensely wealthy one." Lionel gave a lazy smile. He had insisted on getting a bottle of champagne though Sera couldn't quite see what they were celebrating. It felt like the biggest disaster ever.

"Anyway, on to Plan B. This one might take a bit longer but I do have a couple of cards up my sleeve. And a rather brilliant idea, which if it comes off, will do far more than merely see Victoria off." He refused to reveal the tiniest detail about what it was, other than to tell them they would have to be patient.

The waiter brought their main courses. There had been a set lunch menu but Lionel had insisted they order à la carte, though it was twice the price. "There's no point coming all the way up to London to have soup and a roll," he told Sera.

In the end all three of them went for the sirloin which turned out to be the best steak Sera had ever eaten.

Lois, who had been uncharacteristically quiet throughout most of the meal, asked Lionel the question that Sera had burned to ask but hadn't dared. "So what's the deal with Mr Marek and Victoria? How on earth did that happen?"

Lionel put down his fork and sighed. "You might well ask. She's like a praying mantis. She got her hooks into him about ten years ago when he was still an emerging artist. My fault, since I introduced him to her via Maurice. Back in those days she was admittedly rather attractive. Not my type, thank God, but enough to turn heads, Tarq's among them." He took a swig of his champagne.

"Tarq would flay me alive for telling you all this, of course. Anyway she clung to him even more like a limpet as his star rose, she liked to kid herself that his success was the result of her machinations and promotion. It wasn't at all, but she's extremely tenacious when she wants to be. She was already married of course so she and Tarq were always rather on and off," Lionel explained.

Sera dared to ask: "Didn't Maurice mind?"

"He didn't know the half of it, I made sure of that. She put up a pretence that she was mentoring several young artists, helping them with social connections and so on. Maurice may have bought it for a while but I'm sure he eventually saw through it. Then Tarq suffered a bereavement during which Victoria dropped him like a stone for some other young stud, and as you doubtless know he didn't paint for a few years. She had no intention of being around yesterday's news and thankfully vanished from the scene. Until Maurice finally got fed up." Lionel put down his glass. "So there you have it. The sad and sorry saga of an increasingly desperate and predatory woman."

"She can't possibly think blackmailing him into being with her will work?" Lois said.

Lionel shrugged. "Who knows what that mantis thinks? But I'll fix her somehow." He affected a languid look but there was a wicked gleam in his eyes.

Lois excused herself to go to the bathroom and Sera was left alone with Lionel. He dropped his nonchalant, light-hearted manner and became serious. "You realise Tarq's crazy about you, don't you? I've never seen him like this before. The thing with

Victoria was nothing on this. And that painting! He never painted her, I can tell you that."

Sera's stomach did a somersault. "Do you really think so?"

"He's putting up with her because of you. I've also never seen him as aggressive as he was when I came round that time. He might have his moods but he's never been possessive. Normally he'd just laugh. I'm telling you far more than I should, but only because I think it's worth you hanging in there. He's not going to fall for Victoria again. Not now he's fallen so hard for you."

25. Christmas

On Christmas Eve Sera was still awake when there was a noise at her window. Something collided with it.

Fearing Rudolph had bruised his nose she opened the curtains. But it wasn't Father Christmas or his reindeer.

Instead a tall, dark figure stood below, silhouetted against a streetlight. Her heart swelled as she instantly recognised the one person she had missed and longed for these past weeks. What was he doing there? She checked her alarm clock: it was one am.

Sera pulled on a warm jumper and crept downstairs. Everyone else was asleep. She carefully avoided the stair that always creaked and made her way down into the hallway. She was used to this in reverse, as well as opening the front door silently, as when she was returning late from a party or a club she always took care not to wake her family up on her return.

Outside her breath frosted in the air.

"I can't stay, she thinks I'm picking up aspirin from the all-night service station. I wanted to you have this." Mr Marek held out a wrapped, square package.

"I've missed you."

"You're not the only one, baby. But I have to go."

Sera tried to stop him. "Wait!"

He paused.

Not sure how to keep him there she said: "Happy Christmas" and pressed herself into his arms. Put her lips on his, felt the warmth between them in the freezing darkness.

Mr Marek resisted for a moment then yielded. His mouth opened, his tongue entering hers in a kiss that was deep and sweet. Sera felt like she was drinking him in. His arms went around her and for a moment she was locked in his embrace.

He broke off. "The taste of you, the feel. I crave you, Seraphina."

Then he turned and was gone.

Sera felt bereft but she understood the risk. Victoria was probably sitting back at his place with a stopwatch.

Hugging the parcel to her chest she carefully entered the house and returned to her bedroom. She couldn't sleep for hours, thinking of him. Having horrible visions of Victoria forcing her advances on him. They had been a couple before, what if he gave in?

But he came all this way and kissed me, she thought. On Christmas.

* * *

Sera was superstitious about Christmas. When she was very small she had been warned that presents would vanish if she tried to peek or unwrap them before Christmas morning. She no longer believed this but she still avoided ever putting it to the test.

So she went back to bed without unwrapping Mr Marek's parcel. She wanted the full magic of Christmas when she did: that sense of waking up to endless wonderful surprises.

She was also fairly certain that it was a painting of some kind - something framed, anyway - and she would want to see it in the clearest daylight possible not by her bedside lamp.

After what seemed like a dreamless sleep she woke, showered and dressed while she opened the small gifts in the stocking that her parents still hung on her door every year. Her brothers were already racing around the house causing havoc with the various toys they had unwrapped.

Bigger presents came later, under the tree.

Sera slipped downstairs and put Mr Marek's present with the others in the large pile. It would possibly raise some questions, depending on what it was, but she could always claim it was by one of the other students at art class.

"Happy Christmas," her father greeted her, serving up pancakes with smoked salmon. Marisa was sipping Bucks Fizz and offered Sera a glass.

The orange juice and champagne cocktail felt festive and Sera tried to feel glad that she had family around her. Her heart might feel half-broken but at least he was still thinking of her.

"Anyone going to church?" her father asked, knowing full well the answer would be no. The boys were an absolute nightmare on Christmas morning, fired up with sweets and chocolate and wanting to play with their new gifts.

Sera, who liked carols, had half thought about going to the local church but decided it was too cold outside. Besides she was secretly even more keen than the twins to open the main presents.

Finally they were all sitting around the living room, Marisa's parents having arrived to spend the day with them, and the two boys taking it in turns to play "postman".

A new scarf. Some make-up from Lois. Bubble bath. Something from Joel that Sera rapidly buried under other things after seeing the words "Adult Enjoyment" on it.

"What's that, dear?" Marisa's mother asked her.

"Something for styling hair," Sera mumbled, vowing to kill Joel. She had managed to give him a perfectly respectable book on musical theatre, that he'd mentioned wanting.

Then Mr Marek's parcel was finally uncovered. "This one doesn't have a label."

"It's mine," Sera said quickly. "From a friend in art class. The label must have dropped off."

It was handed to her and she opened it carefully, fighting the instinct to rip the paper off as quickly as possible. It was wrapped with string and parcel paper, with a layer of bubble wrap underneath.

She drew it out.

A beautiful oil of a seascape lay before her. A small boat - she recognised it as the same boat in the picture in Mr Marek's home - drifted on much calmer waters.

There were still clouds in the sky: brooding colours of slate, ash and gunmetal. But dawn was breaking on the horizon - a cold, rose gold - and overall it felt like a picture of hope. The craft was waiting for the skies to fully clear.

She could tell from the smell of oils that it was recently painted. How had he hidden it from Victoria?

"That's rather beautiful," Marisa's mother said, looking over her shoulder. "Who's it by?"

"One of the artists in my evening class."

"What a lovely gift. Gives one a rather strange feeling, looking at it. They must be very talented."

Sera carried the painting back to her room and to safety as soon as possible. She didn't want any more questions about it and she didn't want one of the boys damaging it in one of their energetic games. They had already nearly knocked the tree over twice.

She took down a decorative mirror that hung on the wall: it was the wrong height and size to use as a looking glass anyway. Mr Marek's painting replaced it. She wondered if he had titled it but there was no writing on the back. Just his signature in the bottom corner: T. Marek.

Now she could lie and gaze at it and dream of him and what might have been.

* * *

Lois rang later. "Bloody Joel. Did he give you a Rampant Rocket as well? I had to pretend it was a microphone. What the hell was he thinking, with all my elderly relatives there?"

"I had to say it was curling tongs," Sera said. "Do you think you'll use yours?"

"The rate my love life's going, almost certainly," Lois said. "But don't you dare tell Joel. I'm going to tell him I gave it to Oxfam, I don't want him making buzzing noises and sniggering all the time."

Sera agreed. She could only imagine the glee with which Joel would have viewed their embarrassment on opening the presents.

"So what else did you get up to?" Lois asked. "No mistletoe and Mr Marek, I take it."

"No. Well, not exactly. He gave me a present. It's a painting."

Lois was surprised "A painting? What's it of?"

"A seascape," Sera told her.

"Oh. Given he painted you in the nude, I thought he might have painted himself naked, for you. I'd have liked to have seen that."

Sera had seen the flesh-and-blood reality of that and preferred it to any two-dimensional reproduction. "No naked bodies. Just a boat on the sea, but it's really beautiful."

"I wonder how he painted it and got it in the post without Vile Victoria seeing?"

Sera had also wondered the first part of this. "He didn't post it, he dropped it off."

"In person?"

Sera told Lois about the gravel thrown on her window and the midnight meeting.

Lois was impressed. "It's like Wuthering Heights or something. When Heathcliff comes to her window in the night."

English literature was not Lois's strong point. "It's the other way around, she comes to his window. And anyway I wasn't wearing a long white robe or something. I was in my pyjamas and dressing gown."

There was laughter. "Only you could ruin such a romantic scene like that. I would have fled outside in a silken negligée."

"Not at minus two degrees you wouldn't have."

"I would have just got him to warm me up. I take it there wasn't time for that?"

There had barely been time for more than their brief kiss, apparently.

Lois tried to console her. "He probably couldn't risk having your lipstick or scent all over his body."

"I'm not Marilyn Monroe. I don't go to bed with a full face of make-up wearing Chanel No. 5," Sera pointed out.

"Then I suspect he knew he couldn't control himself if he did. One brief kiss and all the suppressed passion he's been feeling all these weeks might have erupted. Any more than one brief kiss and he would have thrown you on the ground and lost all control. Then imagine what your neighbours would say."

146

26. Irresistible

Spring Term. What an ironic descriptor for freezing, leaden-skied early January. There was nothing "spring" about the first day back at school in any sense of the word.

Except for a tiny spring of joy in Sera's heart that she would finally see Mr Marek again. Evening classes at the Community Centre didn't start for another two weeks and she hadn't seen him since that glimpse on Christmas Eve.

He caught her eye a couple of times in art class. He looked haggard, like he had lost weight and not slept for weeks. Sera ached to be with him.

The lesson finished - it was lunch break next - and she lingered.

"Sera." He said her name. They both looked at one another, mutual longing in their eyes.

"I know I should go. I just wanted to thank you for the painting. It's so beautiful," she said.

"I'm glad you liked it."

"It's on my bedroom wall. It reminds me of the other one, but it's so much more hopeful."

Mr Marek was silent, gazing at her. Then he spoke, his voice ragged.

"I need you. I can't take this any more, Sera. I need you. Come here."

She went up to him and he took her in his arms. His mouth came down on hers, first gently, tenderly. Then he was crushing her, his tongue probing her, his hands over her body.

He broke off. "I've got to have you. It's been weeks, I'm going out of my mind."

"You and Victoria...?" Sera was still paranoid that the blonde woman would have inveigled her way back into his bed.

"God no. I've been living like a monk. There's nobody I want but you."

He had never admitted anything like this before and Sera felt her heart melt. "I've missed you so much."

He stroked her cheek. "Me too, baby." He started kissing her again and she could feel his hardness pressing against her.

Then he was leading her across the room towards the storage cupboard. "I know how insanely risky this is but I've got to have you just this once."

Sera was too stunned and turned on to resist.

He closed the door behind them. "Face the wall," he commanded. She obeyed.

Roughly he rucked her skirt up and pulled her underwear aside. He wasn't taking no for an answer. She wanted him so badly his aggression only turned her on more.

She heard him undo his zip. Then in one long, hard, deep thrust he was inside her and she gasped at the shock of it. She was already wet for him so it didn't hurt but he was as deep in her as he had ever been, almost to the point of discomfort.

Sera shifted, changing the angle and he pulled her hips hard against him to keep the depth.

"Christ, you're even better than I remember. I'm not going to last long." He reached round to slip his fingers between her folds, giving her the stimulation she needed to reach her peak simultaneously with him.

Sera's body was fighting her mind. Her mind was freaking out, terrified at what they were doing and the possibility of being discovered. Anyone might walk in at any time.

But her body was a hopeless mass of sensation, wanting more and more of him.

Possibly because he sensed her conflict, he began murmuring things to her that distracted her from her fears. How good she felt. How much he wanted her. How he wasn't going to stop until she gave in. He was relentless. "I have never, ever needed to fuck anyone like I need to fuck you, Seraphina."

Finally she couldn't take it any more and almost sobbing, gave him what he wanted from her. As he felt her contract around him he thrust powerfully into her, taking his own orgasm.

They stood there, Sera's legs feeling weak and wobbly, both wet with heat and out of breath. He leant against her and she felt the heavy weight of him against her back.

"Come June I'm going to tie you to my bed and not let you out for a week," he vowed. "Don't make any plans because the moment school is out, you're mine."

* * *

It got no easier. Mr Marek didn't dare to repeat his behaviour so Sera had to cling on to the hope that if he still wanted her and not Victoria after several weeks of separation, he might be able to hold out until June.

Each lesson was a form of exquisite torture, being near to him but separate from him. She longed for him to command her into the art storage cupboard again but he seemed to have regained his self-control.

So Sera threw herself into her work. Her A-level art project was the most important thing she had done so far, her university application and entire future rested on it. She also put more hours into her other subjects which pleased her teachers.

She was also spending more time with Joel. Lois seemed strangely evasive and Sera wondered whether she felt excluded because she wasn't planning a career in art like the others.

"What's up with Lois?" she asked Joel, after Lois claimed to be doing something else one weekend when there was a party on.

"You tell me. A secret lover, I assume. We should stalk her and find out."

Sera was slightly hurt if Lois was keeping a secret from her but she figured there must be a good reason. Joel was only too happy to reveal every salacious detail of his own colourful love life. He seemed to be dating a different guy every week thanks to his job at Orion.

Jasper's reaction to her A-level artwork project, a portrait of him and Barry in the oils that Tarq had given her, moved Sera more than anything. The theme had been "love" and she had chosen to do a painting of the couple, now celebrating forty years together.

Barry had given her a lot of help and advice with the oils, though she hadn't let him see the final portrait. "Don't overwork them," he had advised her. "Trust the colours."

She had done, and it had worked.

There were tears in Jasper's eyes when Sera finally unveiled it to the evening class.

"When I was a very small boy my godfather took me to the theatre for a birthday treat. We had marvellous seats, at the very front row of the dress circle. When they opened the curtains - I can remember the thick, red velvet as it parted to reveal all the brightness and colour inside - I felt that they were opening a huge birthday present just for me. Bright and glittering, with these marvellous scenes within. Throughout the entire show, I thought the actors were performing solely for me. It was only when it finished and the whole audience applauded that I realised it was for other people as well."

He turned to Sera. "This is how your painting make me feel. As though I am the only person in the world seeing it. As though the world, for a moment, has stopped just for me."

His voice was gruffer on these last words, losing its usual silken theatrical smoothness.

By some trick of the light and the way Sera had painted it, you could see the beauty of the two young men they had once been. The underlying bone structure seemed stronger than the lines and marks of age and time giving character to the older faces above it.

Their personalities were there: the painting revealed more than a mirror. Jasper's face displayed its wit, mischief and charm, but there was a vulnerability in his eyes. Barry, whose features were softer, his eyes a gentler pale blue, showed a quiet strength. It was an honest portrait yet also a compassionate one.

"It's just absolutely exquisite," Elizabeth said. "You've more than captured them. It's more real than either of you," she said, looking to Jasper and Barry.

"It's... just right," Barry said slowly. This was all he said, but Sera could see that he was deeply moved and it moved her as well.

They all stood in silence for a few moments, each thinking their own thoughts.

Mr Marek came up behind them. "The struggle you now face," he told Sera, "is losing confidence that you will ever paint anything like this again. But I can assure you that you will."

"Is it good then?" Sera asked. "Do you like it?"

Mr Marek considered the painting for a few more moments and returned his gaze to Sera. "It's a masterpiece," he said simply. Then he smiled at her, one of his rare, kind smiles that momentarily made her feel that he saw her as an equal, as a fellow artist.

Sera felt dizzy. She took a deep breath.

"There are things that in five or ten years you may do differently. Small changes to your technique, the use of the palette knife. But while these may make it more perfect in a technical sense, the absence of them doesn't reduce the impact of your work," Mr Marek told her.

It was more than he had said directly to her in weeks. When would this ordeal be over?

Joel had also done brilliantly. He had created a kind of tableau with a painted backdrop of Shakespeare's The Tempest. Four art figurines clad in exquisitely designed miniature costumes were posed in front of it: Prospero, Miranda, Caliban and Ariel.

Lois had produced a pop-art work in the style of Andy Warhol. Instead of cans of beans she had painted Joel's Christmas gift, in nine different squares like Warhol's Monroe.

It sparked some outrage at St Christopher's. "It's self-love, isn't it?" Lois had defended her work. Fortunately Mr Marek took a more progressive view than Mr Billings would have done and didn't try to prevent her from entering it.

Lois caused further outrage by acting as a living canvas for Janette's project. She wore a flesh coloured bikini and Janette covered her in bright, rainbow body paints, photographing the result. Mr Marek had managed to verify with the Exam Board that a painted human would qualify.

27. The gallery

There was a red spot on the top corner of Mr Marek's painting of Sera. Someone had already bought it.

For some reason this crushed her though she knew she should have felt happy for him that it had sold so quickly.

It was the first time that she, Lois and Joel had been to a gallery opening. They were all dressed up to the nines. The evening class students had also been given invitations and all of them had made it, even Bob and Winifred.

"You are a dark horse," Jasper commented to Sera when she had told him about the painting. They were all fascinated that Sera had secretly been posing for him.

"We had to keep it discreet because my school probably wouldn't have approved," Sera explained. This was as true as anything. Her parents would also have freaked out, in fact they still would once they discovered what had been going on. She was going to have to brace herself for that conversation.

"He's certainly done a very beautiful job," Elizabeth said. "Of course you're naturally very lovely, Sera, he hasn't painted anything that isn't there. It was rather a shame we couldn't finish sketching you that first week, I've always thought. But there's something quite magical about this painting, isn't there? The quality of the winter light streaming through, and the glowing ruby of the drape over the couch."

Sera confessed that she struggled to feel comfortable looking at her unclothed self.

"That's only natural, dear. Were it me up there - even in my heyday - I would have pinned my handkerchief over certain areas by now," Winifred said.

It wasn't merely the nudity. It was also being an object. Sera was the object of the painting that everyone wanted to see and it made her feel oddly removed from herself. As though she didn't own her own image any more.

Lionel had fixed up the exhibition opening night to be a momentous occasion. The champagne flowed, endless caviar and other delicacies travelled round the room on silver trays and a harpist in a diaphanous gown played a mellow tune on a small dais.

Lionel was also brilliant with the art press: they danced to his tune. It helped that he had an uncanny eye for talent spotting and kept uncovering the Next Big Things.

Tonight he was barely suppressing his delight as he greeted Sera, Lois and Joel. "I may as well tell you all now. We've had a two hundred and fifty thousand pound bid for Tarq's painting of Sera." He said this in deliberate earshot of a couple of journalists who immediately hovered closer.

"Is that why there's a red dot on it?" Lois asked.

"Partly. We haven't confirmed the sale yet but the offer came in this afternoon. From a buyer in Japan who already owns several Mareks. A buyer with quite exceptional taste to choose a work of this beauty and quality," Lionel said in a subtly louder tone, angling for the critics to quote his remark.

Sera wasn't sure how she felt about such a huge offer. It was a huge amount to take in. The thought of some unknown Japanese man forever gazing upon her naked form was more unsettling than she had realised it would be.

She didn't have long to think about this because at that moment an icily furious Victoria accosted her. She looked devastatingly stylish in a slinky silvery garment which would have had two extra zeroes on its price tag than Sera's frock had. Large emeralds glittered at her throat, though Joel muttered "paste" behind Sera's ear.

"Exactly what are you doing here?"

"I was invited by Lionel," Sera told her.

"You know the agreement. You stay well away or there will be consequences."

Sera could finally see what Joel had perceived about Victoria's age. She was very well preserved and her make-up was immaculate, but there was no way she was in her late thirties. For a split second Sera almost pitied the other woman her desperation.

But then she caught sight of Mr Marek's face and the haunted look on his face, and her heart hardened against Victoria's machinations.

Lionel rapidly intervened. "Victoria, darling, some people you must meet. We needed the model here for publicity purposes, nothing more," he said to appease her, casting an apologetic glance Sera's way.

Victoria glared at Sera as the gallery owner ushered her away.

"That was close," Lois said.

Sera was fretting. "Do you think she'll tell?"

Joel doubted it. "She'll lose him the moment she does. I think she just wanted you out of the picture so he'd focus on her again."

It hadn't worked of course. It may have kept them apart, except for those couple of lapses, but the forced separation had only made Sera feel even more strongly about her art teacher.

Tonight they were thrown into proximity by the occasion and there was nothing Victoria could do about it. Many people wanted photographs of artist and model together, either side of the painting. Sera's face began to ache from smiling.

Lionel had shielded her from any interviews lest the newspapers unearthed the somewhat scandalous circumstances of their teacher-pupil relationship. Even if nothing further than modelling was suspected between them, it would still cause a sensation for a school art teacher to have painted a nude portrait of his sixth form student. So when any inquiries were made, Lionel implied that Sera was a professional model.

Sera got just a few minutes alone with Mr Marek when Victoria visited the powder room. She had stuck to him like glue all evening but could hardly drag him into the ladies' with her.

"I can't believe the price offered," Sera said.

"That's Lionel for you. He wasn't a bad artist when we were at art school but selling art turned out to be his true talent." He dropped his voice. "I still miss you, baby. Wait for me." He looked devastatingly handsome that night in a well cut suit.

As if she could do anything but wait. "I miss you too."

He paused, drinking her in. There was hunger in his eyes. "That painting, it's what you did to me."

Sera was puzzled. "This one?"

"The boat. You took me out of the storms." He was gazing at her so sincerely, a strange and tender look on his face, that her stomach dissolved. She couldn't speak.

She just wanted to be in his arms. For the whole room and everyone in it to disappear. Looking at him, she felt that he was thinking the same.

All too soon Victoria returned and whisked her reluctant escort away once again, leaving Sera by herself. Joel was the other side of the room chatting up a handsome young artist. Her fellow art class students were grouped in one corner of the room nibbling canapés. Jasper was giving her a somewhat knowing look, having observed her conversation with Mr Marek.

Lois was nowhere to be seen.

Feeling like taking a break herself, Sera slipped out the back of the gallery. There was a service and utility area outside where the caterers had their trolleys and there was a goods lift. Sera was about to walk around the corner when she stopped short.

There was a couple pressed up against the opposite wall.

It was Lionel, locked in a passionate embrace with Lois.

* * *

The rest of the evening passed in a bit of a blur. Sera decided to pretend she hadn't seen anything although she intended to give Lois a huge grilling later on.

She had hardly been able to believe her eyes. Lionel had seemed so uninterested in Lois when they met for lunch in London, and Lois had barely said a single word about him. Sera had at least expected her to comment on Lionel's looks but she had been very non-committal.

How had this happened?

When Lionel returned to the room he was as suave and debonair as ever, working the room and promoting the various artists.

156

"Just wait until the papers come out. It will all be fixed up then, darling," he said as he passed her.

Sera was puzzled. "What do you mean?"

"You'll see." For some reason Lionel delighted in being cryptic.

They were driving back in two cars: Bob's and Barry's. Lois ended up in Bob's car while Sera and Joel went in Barry's.

Sera had the strong suspicion that Lois was avoiding her but now at least she had a good idea as to why.

* * *

"Someone wants to paint you for a quarter of a million pounds?" Her father was incredulous. Sera had no choice but to tell them at breakfast the next morning because the price offer was so sensational it was going to be all over the news.

Sera had to correct him. "No, they want to buy a painting that's already been painted of me for that money."

"What painting? Surely not something one of your friends did? Is this some kind of joke, Sera?" Her father looked confused and annoyed, he clearly couldn't take it in.

How could she explain? "I posed for an actual artist. I wasn't sure if it would come out well, so I didn't like to say anything," she told him.

"What artist?"

"His name is Tarquin Marek. He's the guy that teaches at the community centre. He's a professional artist, he's exhibited at the Royal Academy." Sera hoped this might impress and assuage her parents, since there was worse to come and they'd find out everything sooner or later.

Marisa surveyed her with a suspicious glance. "Exactly how did he paint you?"

Sera swallowed. There was no way she could lie, because they were going to see the painting. Everyone was going to see the damn painting because Lionel had rung up every art journalist he knew to brag about the bid. It would be in all the papers in a day or so.

"You know, in a traditional pose."

Marisa's voice was calm but hard. "I don't know, Sera. What do you mean by traditional? Was this a nude painting?"

The fiery embarrassment on Sera's face said it all. She couldn't even look at her father.

"For heaven's sake, Sera, what were you thinking? Imagine trying to get a job in a top law or accounting firm with something like that following you around." Marisa was exasperated, totally overlooking Sera's actual career aims once again.

"It's art, it's not dirty," Sera said in protest. "It was very classic, like Renoir or something. Besides I want to be an artist not a business executive. Doing this has been really good experience."

Her father was firmly on Marisa's side. "He must be an absolute scoundrel to talk a young girl into exposing herself like that. If I ever get my hands on him..."

Sera was quick to interrupt. "He's not a scoundrel, he's a really nice man. Really talented."

"That remains to be seen," her father said.

"At least wait until you've seen the painting. It's really not as bad as you're imagining."

What had really gone on was far worse than they were imagining but Sera was sparing them that knowledge for the moment.

28. Headlines

The next day the story of the quarter million pound painting broke and a huge bouquet of flowers arrived from Lionel with a two-word message:

"Respectability restored."

Sera was beginning to realise what he meant. The enormous price had elevated the painting from a "dirty daub" as Joel had phrased it to something considered an internationally acclaimed work of exceptional quality.

It meant that day at school - even though she faced the excruciating embarrassment of everyone having seen her naked - the general consensus was awe rather than condemnation. St Christopher's could hardly expel a student of adult age who had been featured in a *"modern masterpiece that heralds a 20th century Renaissance"* according to the Telegraph.

The fact this was actually a quote lifted directly from Lionel, faithfully repeated by a love-struck critic who had made a pass at the gallery owner, was not disclosed.

Lionel had played his trump card and won.

The painting being a nude also boosted interest. "It gives them a free pass to put Page Three on the front page," Lionel had said. "Not that you're Page Three, darling, you're far more beautiful and refined. But tits, at the end of the day, are tits to the tabloids."

And so a story that might have remained confined to the broadsheets was all over the mid-market and gutter press as well. The worst was the Daily Mail: *"Would you pay £250k for this girl?"*

"The answer to those headlines is always 'no'," Joel said, "only in this case someone clearly decided they would pay that."

A couple of the papers had photographs of Sera standing by Mr Marek, but even more had photos of him and the ghastly Victoria. Sera was dismayed how well Victoria photographed. The Daily Mail had a whole paragraph on the *"glamorous former model Victoria Venables, recently separated from husband and well-known art patron Maurice Venables, on the arm of Tarquin Marek"*.

"It makes it sound like the Maurice guy is dating Marek," Lois said. "It's not very well written, is it?"

"I imagine he'd rather date old Maurice than that vampire," Joel remarked. "I know I would."

"Obviously you would. You'd rather date him than me as well. Or Sera."

Joel gave an expression of mock thoughtfulness. "Yes, I rather think I would. Quite apart from the matter of appendages he's apparently spectacularly rich."

Better still there was no mention of Sera being Mr Marek's student so the reputation of St Christopher's remained, for now, intact. Sera feared that it could still slip out in future and kept her fingers mentally crossed that no journalists would find out.

She was nonetheless summoned to the headmaster. He was a creepy little man with a mousy moustache and an unctuous voice. His office always smelt of stale coffee and talcum powder, bizarrely.

Sera was told to take a chair. This was a good sign as if you were facing the music you were forced to stand.

"I expect you know why I've called you here," he began. "While we wouldn't normally condone this sort of activity, I understand that it is your own ambition to become an artist and that you currently take drawing classes with Mr Marek outside school. I imagine this project emanated from that and has been a form of work experience."

So that was how they had decided to tolerate with it, Sera thought. By considering it to be something external to the school.

The headmaster continued. "To date the school has fortunately not been mentioned and it would be preferable all round if this was to remain the case. While you may be eighteen and of legal age to model, awkward questions may still be raised to the board of governors by concerned parents. So for everyone's

160

sake it would be best not to have St Christopher's named in association with this."

He had spoken his prepared, stuffy little speech. Wisely Sera kept her response demure, thanking the headmaster for his understanding. She wondered whether they would be summoning Mr Marek as well-but didn't dare ask.

The painting was naturally the talk of the school all day. Quite a few girls were envious as they had crushes on the art teacher.

"Wasn't it weird seeing him in class after doing that?" "What's his house like?" "Did he ever try anything?"

Sera managed to fend off most of the more compromising questions. She explained that it had come about through evening classes, which it had really, and had been a purely professional arrangement.

"So how much were you paid?" "Oh my God I wonder if he'd paint me!"

One girl called her a skanky slut and some of the boys made boob jokes in front of her. Generally it wasn't as bad as it might have been and Sera survived it.

* * *

That left one more person to tackle.

"What the hell was going on last night? With you and Lionel?"

Lois tried to bluff her way out of it. "I have no idea what you mean."

"I saw you both. Out the back. You weren't pushing a trolley of canapés."

Lois scrunched up her eyes as though she had a headache. "I didn't want to tell you given everything you're going through with Mr Marek. And I barely know how it happened. I went to that lunch and it was like a coup de foudre as they say in France. A lightning strike. Lust at first sight. He's exactly my type, you must know that."

Sera didn't know. "I get that he's blond but he looks nothing like George Peppard or any of the boys you've ever dated."

"That's because I've never had access to a man like that. There's no one remotely like him at school or in town, is there? They don't make them like that here."

"So how did it happen. Did he call you?" Sera asked.

Lois explained. "You remember he gave us both his business cards. Well when he gave me mine he kind of brushed his thumb over my fingers and gave me this look. So I called him a few days later, I didn't even have a clue what to say, but he said he'd hoped I'd call and it just went from there."

"Went from there to where? You haven't slept with him, have you?"

Lois looked slightly shamefaced. "Just once. Honestly, Sera, it was amazing. He really knew what he was doing."

This was no surprise to Sera. "He comes across as a bit of a playboy. I should think he's had plenty of practice."

"Anyway you can hardly condemn me, given what you're doing. Or would be doing were it not for Vicky the bitch."

It was true. "I only want you to be happy, Lois. He might chew you up and spit you out."

"He might. And I might be quite ecstatic if he did." Lois had a dreamy look on her face that Sera knew meant trouble. She couldn't help but feel envious of Lois and the freedom she effectively had compared to Sera.

If only Mr Marek hadn't been her damn teacher.

But he was, and the thought of him meting out his unique style of discipline after class made Sera shiver.

29. Vanquished

Later that week Lionel insisted on driving up from London and taking everyone to a celebratory dinner. Sera suspected his goal was also to see Lois but she kept her thoughts to herself. He had invited both of them but she didn't see how she could go if Mr Marek and Victoria were both going as well.

He picked them both up from Lois's place in his silver sports car. Sera gallantly offered to sit in the back as she knew Lois would want the front seat but it was horribly uncomfortable, there was no leg-room and her knees were practically squashed up to her chin.

She could see why Mr Marek, who was a couple of inches taller than Lionel, drove a regular sedan. Sports cars were tiny inside.

They drove up to Mr Marek's house, Sera feeling increasingly nervous and wondering what the hell Lionel was playing at. Victoria would be furious. Why was he fanning the flames?

"Are you sure this is a good idea?" she asked when he moved the seat forward for her to get out. At least if she stayed in the car until the restaurant Victoria might make less of a scene there.

Lionel flashed her a smile. "It's a perfectly excellent idea."

Being inside Mr Marek's house brought everything flooding back. She realised it was several months since she had been there. The familiar smell of oils mingling with plants in the conservatory drifted through. She saw his easel from a distance and wondered what he was currently painting.

There was also a horrid cloying scent of some designer fragrance fighting with the aroma of art and coffee. Doubtless Victoria. That woman had infused this place like a horrible coiling serpent, wrapping herself around Mr Marek and his life and squeezing out Sera.

"Lionel, Lois, Sera." Was it her imagination or did he linger on her name? "Great to see you, we're just about ready. Anyone like a drink before we go?"

Lionel declined on their behalf. "The restaurant wouldn't take a booking later than eight and threatened me with all sorts of doom lest we arrive after then."

Victoria sailed into the room. She was wearing evening trousers and an emerald satin blouse with huge frilly puffed shoulders. On anyone else it would have looked absurd and fussy but as an ex-model, she carried it off perfectly. Her frosted hair seemed huger than ever.

Sera, wearing her only other evening dress that wasn't the one she had worn to the gallery, felt eclipsed.

Victoria narrowed her eyes. "I might have been forced to tolerate this piece at the gallery, Lionel, but I'm as sure as hell not suffering her in my own home."

Sera wanted to sink through the floor.

Mr Marek's expression was inscrutable. Lionel's was relaxed and amused. "Aren't you?"

"You know the deal. She leaves now or I phone her school first thing in the morning." Her narrowed eyes shot hatred at Sera's.

"Feel free to try," Lionel said.

Victoria spun back to him. "I beg your pardon?"

"Feel free to try. They already know about the painting from the newspapers and it has been no issue," he told her.

"I hardly imagine they'll be as delighted to discover what else has been going on." Malice twisted Victoria's face.

Sera was feeling sick with fear. She had dreaded this happening more than anything, why was Lionel provoking the woman?

But he remained unruffled just as Mr Marek remained impassive. "Exactly what has been going on?" Lionel asked.

"You know full well," Victoria snapped.

"All I know is that you've been living with Tarq since last November and as far as the rest of the world is aware, the two of you are together. You've shot yourself in the foot, my dear. What shred of evidence do you have that he's been seeing Sera or anyone else? Hundreds of witnesses can attest that you've clung to him like a limpet for months."

Her hands clenched into claws from fury, Victoria spat her words at him. "You know perfectly well what was going on between them."

"So far as I, the rest of the art world and the press are concerned, nothing more than a perfectly professional artist-model arrangement ever took place. Tarq even kept records of payments which his accountant would be happy to produce. If you try to make trouble you'll merely look like a woman scorned stirring up lies out of desperation." Lionel cast a glance at Mr Marek. "For scorned - if I may take the liberty of announcing it, Tarq? - is exactly what you are. I suggest you pack your bags."

"Paying that little whore who would have given it up for free, to you and half the artists in England I'll warrant!"

Mr Marek stepped forward. "That's enough." His calm tone masked deep anger. "It's over. Not that it ever restarted, as you well know. You can stay here tonight but then you're gone."

"Tarquin!" Victoria's tone was a mixture of shock, disbelief and pleading.

"I've tolerated you for Sera's sake but she's safe now. There's no point making a scene. It's time you went back to London."

"And leave you here with that scheming little hussy?" Victoria's voice was rising in fury.

The art teacher ignored the insinuation. "What I do is none of your business. Thinking you could blackmail your way into any long term position in my life was deranged, Victoria."

The blonde woman looked desperately from him to Lionel and back but saw no pity and no yielding. She at least knew when she was thwarted. Tilting her chin in a defiant manner, she announced: "You're deranged if you think I would join you for dinner tonight after this insult."

Lionel gave a brief laugh. "The restaurant is booked for four people. You were never invited in the first place. While we're gone you'll have time to gather your things and be ready for the taxi I'm ordering, courtesy of the Gallery as my farewell gift to you, to take you to the station first thing tomorrow."

Victoria stormed out.

There were a few moments of silence, broken by Lois. "Jesus," she murmured.

Sera was in absolute shock and turmoil. Confusion mixed with relief and hope and uncertainty. Did this mean that she and Mr Marek...? She could hardly ask that in front of the others. There were so many things she was burning to know. "How come you didn't tell me?" she asked Mr Marek.

"Lionel insisted on having the privilege of finally telling her where to go," Mr Marek - now Tarq again, she supposed - told her.

Lionel grinned. "I've been wanting to see that Gorgon off ever since she started getting her claws into my artists. But my business relationship with Maurice forced me to remain civil to her. Now he's washed his hands of her, I can finally tip her down the drain where she belongs."

The four of them headed off to the restaurant, taking the art teacher's car as it seated everyone more comfortably.

"What if she slashes all your stuff while you're out?" Lois asked him.

He shrugged. "Clothes are clothes. They can be replaced."

"I mean your paintings?"

"I've barely been able to paint while she's been there. I have a couple of canvases I'm working on in free periods at St Christopher's."

Sera wondered about the stormy seascape.

Tarq twisted around to look at her in the back seat. "It's in London. I took it down the same day you left." His eyes conveyed what he couldn't say in front of the others.

"London?" Lois asked, oblivious to the unspoken exchange between him and Sera.

"I have a flat there," he explained.

"Whereabouts?"

"Russell Square. Bloomsbury."

Over dinner, at the most expensive restaurant in town, they were still discussing Victoria. Sera was glad that Lionel had taken charge of the wine list as if the Burgundy he ordered cost as much as she feared, she would have struggled to drink it. The menu didn't even have prices on which was stressful in itself.

Sera had never socialised with seriously wealthy people before and hadn't even been aware of Tarq being so well off. From her vague knowledge of London she knew that Russell Square was an extremely upmarket address. When they'd visited Lois's sister once or twice it seemed that everyone lived miles from the centre, an hour out on the Northern line in shared houses where even the living rooms were converted into bedrooms.

To actually own a flat in central London was a whole different league of existence. But given paintings sold for six figures, perhaps it was no wonder. Still, it was hard to come to terms with.

Lois voiced her thoughts. "I can't get my head around all of this. I mean a quarter of a million quid for a painting? Not that it wasn't really nice, of course."

Tarq and Lionel exchanged a glance. "Sometimes the market and buyers can be unpredictable," Lionel said.

Sera worked her way through quail ballantine, filet mignon and a lemon soufflé. The men also had a cheese course but she was too full to eat any. Finally there was coffee and a plate of petits-fours. Lois ate most of them.

As they left Tarq slipped his arm across her back, guiding her down the steps. He walked her a few paces away from Lionel and Lois who were discussing a film.

He turned her around and gazed down at her. He cupped her face in his hands. "Come and stay with me tonight. Waiting to be with you has been killing me and I can't waste another night."

"But what about Victoria?" Her presence in the house would hardly be conducive to passion.

"I mean in London. We can drive up there tonight."

"But it's miles!"

He tilted her face up towards his and brushed her lips lightly with a kiss. "We'll be there by midnight. I need you in my bed with me, my darling, all mine."

30. Russell Square

It was a long dark drive down the motorway to London. Sera was still pinching herself. Just a few hours ago she had still been out in the cold, not allowed any contact with Tarq, and the next moment she was going to spend the night with him in London.

Her parents thought she was staying with Lois so that was all good.

Sera felt too nervous to speak much during the journey and Tarq seemed intensely focused on the road. She stole a glance at his profile once or twice and wondered what he was thinking.

As they approached the outskirts of the capital he broke the silence. "We should have a fairly clear run this time of night. We'll be there before long."

London was always surprisingly compact and narrow once you got into the centre. Sera had no idea how anyone drove around the city with all its one-way streets and confusing junctions. She recognised a few places as they drove through to Bloomsbury. She hadn't been to Russell Square that she could remember, but the streets around it seemed like so many other London streets: tall square terraces of elegant houses with black ironwork railing, trees that were dark and shadowy at this hour.

"It's on the top floor, no lift I'm afraid."

They climbed up several flights of stairs to what was the fifth or sixth storey, Sera lost count. Tarq unlocked the door and ushered her inside. He didn't turn the lights on, instead taking her in his arms and kissing her. She melted against him.

"I've been waiting far too long for this. Let's go straight to bed."

Although Sera had been in his bed before she was suddenly nervous. She felt out of her depth here: in a strange flat, all the way in London, with a man she adored but had been at a distance from the past few months.

Tarq sensed her hesitation. "It's okay, baby, I can just hold you. I know it's been a while."

"I do want to be with you," she told him. "It's just..."

"I understand. We can take it as slow as you need. That you're finally here with me is the most important thing."

He wanted her naked in bed with him so peeled off her clothes gradually. Sera unbuttoned his shirt and smoothed her hands over the firm muscles of his torso. He always felt so warm and strong. Despite her nerves she felt safe with him.

"Lie back."

She complied, her head on the pillow.

Tarq moved down her body and pushed her thighs apart. Before Sera could react he had brought his mouth down upon her. It was the first time he had done this to her but he knew exactly what to do. She cried out as his tongue swirled around her button.

He seemed to go for ages, she twisted her hands in his hair as he pleasured her. A couple of times she tried to pull him upwards to her, worried that he would get bored and wanting to reciprocate, but his hands grasped her hips firmly and he remained down there.

After a while Sera was starting to whimper as he forced her towards orgasm. Before it could happen though he moved back over her and swiftly drove into her.

It was enough to bring her over the edge instantly. She clung to him, half-dizzy from desire, letting the waves ripple through her while he maintained a steady rhythm.

He whispered things in her ear that would have made her face flame in daylight. How hard she had made him. How much he loved fucking her. How he wanted to make love to her all night, to tie her down and claim her. He grasped her wrists as he said this, holding them above her head as though he were restraining her.

Not that she needed any restraints. She was more than his.

On the occasions they had slept together before Tarq had got Sera to climax at the same time as he did, but this time he had deliberately brought her off first. After a few minutes of his continued smooth strokes she realised why. He was building her up to it again.

Sera didn't think her body could get worked up and respond again this quickly but he knew it better than she did. He was grinding into her relentlessly and everything that had been over-sensitive and stimulated a few moments ago was already getting fired up again.

It didn't take long. The second time was even more intense than the first, her whole body shook.

She was so tired and it was so overwhelming that she slipped into a deep sleep soon after and didn't remember him finally withdrawing from her, rolling onto his side, and cradling her in his arms throughout the night.

* * *

Sun streamed through the garret windows as Sera woke in Tarq's arms the next morning. She felt safe. She felt home.

She decided to try a little attention of her own and kissed his chest, wriggling down to try and wake him in a particular way.

Just as her mouth closed over him he woke and groaned. "Sera..."

But he let her carry out what she was doing for a while before he pulled her back up, threw her over and finished inside her.

She loved his urgency, his need for her.

Afterwards he showed her the bathroom so she could shower. Sera couldn't help having a quick glance around to see if there were any trace of Victoria. She trusted Tarq in that nothing had happened, she had seen the genuine dislike on his face when he finally got rid of the blonde woman, but maybe Victoria had stayed here? There were other bedrooms.

But there was nothing that indicated a recent female presence. A single toothbrush, male bath products only. Sera supposed Victoria could have used Tarq's but she looked like the kind of woman who would have had her own ultra-expensive brands.

Victoria was definitely someone who liked to establish her presence: Sera had noticed several feminine touches at Tarq's other house the previous evening.

There was no fresh food in the house so they went out for breakfast to a nearby café. Both of them had worked up an appetite again.

"You don't think your stuff will get trashed, do you?" Sera asked him. She had been troubled by Lois's suggestion.

"I doubt it. She'd want to do something worse than that if she did plan on revenge. But I think she knows she's beaten."

Sera hoped so but remained uneasy. She played with a couple of croissant crumbs on her plate.

Tarq tried to reassure her. "Besides, she's well aware of all the business Lionel and Maurice do. One bad word from Lionel and Maurice will play even tougher with the divorce settlement. As it stands he probably plans to be reasonably generous, if for no other reason than to see the back of her."

There was something else that niggled Sera. She wasn't sure how to phrase it. "Was she... very persistent?"

His eyes glinted with amusement as he guessed what she was trying to ask. "You mean did she try to pick the lock on my door or slip me a Mickey Finn? No, it was more about appearances for her. She's not in love with me, she just wanted the status. Then she could claim that she'd run out on her husband rather than been sent packing."

"She wasn't trying to make him jealous?" Sera asked.

Tarq tore open a packet of sugar and poured half into his coffee. He picked up a spoon and stirred the fragrant black liquid. "Have you heard the term 'lavender marriage'?"

Now Sera felt embarrassed for not guessing this before. It tallied with a couple of remarks that Lionel had made, as well explained why Maurice hadn't thrown Victoria out when she first started sleeping around. Then she had a sudden concern.

"Lionel... he isn't... as well...?"

Tarq laughed.

"Good God no. Though he's quite prepared to give any impression if he senses it will win him a business deal or a favourable review. Are you worried about Lois?"

"A little," Sera admitted.

"Don't be. He's smitten." He took her hand and looked into her eyes. "And he's not the only one."

"Really?"

"Absolutely. You're the first girl I've ever taken here. I inherited the flat after my mother died, an elderly uncle had left it to her. I planned to set up a studio in there as the light's not bad in the second south-west facing bedroom. But then I stopped painting," he told her.

Sera remembered what he had said to her when he had showed her the stormy seascape. "Until now."

"Until seeing you naked on that community centre couch awoke every single instinct within me." The heat in his eyes told her that these instincts were not solely artistic.

* * *

The route back took them past Russell Square Underground station, just a stone's throw from Tarq's flat.

"It's only one stop to Saint Martins on the tube from here," Sera said. She had no idea where she would get student accommodation next year, probably miles out, but at least her college would be nearby.

And if he ever invited her to stay the night, something she fervently hoped, it would be a very easy commute the next morning.

Tarq didn't say anything and she wondered if he had understood. "It would make it easier to meet up." She hoped this wasn't presumptuous. "I mean when we're both in London next year."

Still he said nothing and now Sera felt slightly anxious. Maybe he didn't really have any intentions towards her. He had spoken of June and wanting to see her then, but perhaps all he had in mind was a summer romance? Or a fling?

His demeanour now didn't seem to match his words before. Or had she come on too strong? She wished she hadn't said anything. An irrational fear ran through her mind that maybe she hadn't been good enough in bed?

This fear was assuaged half an hour later when he absolutely ravished her body leaving them both exhausted and sated.

"I suppose you can put your studio in now," she said as they lay there.

"Perhaps." He sounded non-committal. He looked lost in thought.

Sera was really getting mixed signals from him and it was making her panic. But pushing for a response and getting nothing made her feel even worse. She remembered how he had seemed to find it so easy to switch off and treat her with cool detachment in class.

Could it be that he could turn off his emotions just as easily? Did "smitten" imply something intense but temporary?

When he drove them back home an hour or so later the atmosphere had grown horribly awkward between them. Sera wondered what on earth she had done.

31. Confessing

Now the aftershocks of the painting story had worn off and she'd gone so far as to spend the night with Tarq in London, Sera decided she was going to have to confess the rest.

"There's something I need to tell you," she began. Marisa was preparing dinner and her father was sitting at the dinner table, not yet laid, trying to fix some odd piece of machinery. It was a typically domestic scene and she was reluctant to shatter their peace.

"It's about the artist who painted me."

Marisa, slicing carrots, tried to second guess her. "He wants you to pose for him again, I assume?"

"Not that. Well, maybe some time, I don't know." It was now or never. "The thing is, we're sort of dating." *I'm having the most amazing, passionate affair of my life and I'm madly, hopelessly in love. Even if I'm not really sure where I stand, a small voice reminded her.*

Both of her parents' jaws nearly hit the floor at this point. Sera couldn't meet their eyes. She had dreaded their reaction and it was even worse than she had feared.

"You're dating your art teacher?" Marisa was horrified and incredulous. "If it wasn't bad enough him compromising you by getting you to pose for him in the first place..."

Sera protested. "He hardly compromised me. He's featured me in an amazing artwork, I mean there are people who would pay tens of thousands of pounds to be painted by someone like him."

"Exactly how old is this man?" Marisa asked, in a tone of pure ice. She reminded Sera of frosty Victoria without the vampiness.

"He's older than me, but I'm eighteen and an adult, so it doesn't matter, does it? It's not like he's any more likely to get me pregnant or break my heart or whatever else than if he was the

174

same age as me, is it? And Dad's several years older than you." She was getting defiant now: defensive, but also genuinely angry and a bit scared that they were treating the news like this.

"That is not the point. I wasn't a schoolgirl when I met your father, I was a mature, independent woman well established in my career. You're still at school. And he's your teacher!"

Sera's father practically had his head in his hands. "Is it something we've done, love? That this man could use you in this way?"

Sera's anger melted, replaced by contrition that her father was actually hurt by this. "It's nothing you've done. He hasn't used me, I'm happier than I've ever been. He's even helped me with my university application and everything."

"It's not right. We'll have to call your school. He should be sacked," Marisa insisted.

"If you do that they'll expel me too and then I won't be able to sit my A-levels and I'll be really screwed," Sera pointed out.

She had them over a barrel.

Her father looked resigned. "We'd better meet him then. And if I find out he's mistreating you in any way..."

Sera pre-empted him. "He's not. You'd know if he was, because I'd be unhappier, and I'm on top of the world. We're taking it slowly for now anyway. I'm not about to move in with him."

"God forbid!"

Little did they know that Tarq had pretty much deliberately avoided suggesting anything of the sort. His weird silence still stung. He had kissed Sera tenderly and arranged to take her out the following weekend but there was still nothing concrete in terms of his future plans.

"And I've got my place at Saint Martins so that's all set. I know you're both worried about me doing Fine Art but if I can't make a go of it, I'll get a job and do a business course at night school." It was the biggest compromise she had ever offered. She had thought they would both be mollified but Marisa looked even more concerned.

"That's hardly going to set you on the path for a top career, is it? The big London firms take graduates from the top universities. You won't have a hope of that," Marisa said.

Sera decided there was no point repeating yet again that she had no plans whatsoever of a corporate career. If she couldn't do art then she would do something else a bit different. Horticulture, even, like Elizabeth. That had always sounded very interesting.

At least Marisa cared enough about her to want her to kind of follow in her footsteps. She could have focused on her sons but she showed just as much concern for Sera's future.

"Dad never did all that, and he still made it." It wasn't as though Marisa had married some hot shot city executive after all. Sera's father was hugely successful but he'd done all his diplomas through sandwich and correspondence courses.

"I suppose so." Marisa still looked dissatisfied but she didn't protest any further.

* * *

They'd had a few more dates but Tarq was still evasive and non-committal about next year. Sera had hoped to talk with him about Saint Martins as both he and Lionel had graduated from there but he always ended up changing the subject.

She had thought he would have been proud of her winning a place there. He had always seemed so supportive of her art. But it increasingly felt like a taboo subject.

So she stopped mentioning it. She tried to talk about other subjects but conversation often felt brittle. There was this huge, great, unspoken thing between them and they both knew it. But only Tarq knew why.

Sera avoided asking him to dinner with her parents as she was sure they would pick up on the tensions. Her father might even become more convinced that he was right about Tarq using her.

Was he using her? Did he only want her body, on a temporary basis?

But between the sheets it was a different world. He was passionate, commanding, demanding: sometimes so much so that it almost scared her. He pushed her to her limits but it always took her to a higher, better place.

Above all Sera felt cherished in bed. The things Tarq murmured to her sounded genuine. It wasn't as though he had to say those things to get her into bed.

And the way he held her afterwards. The way he always insisted on her staying the full night with him. Her parents had probably guessed by now that Sera wasn't really staying at Lois's house but they didn't say anything.

Then there was the pressure of having to remain super discreet at school. It was all starting to become a bit much.

Sera wasn't sure how much longer she could cope with the intense joys and crashing fears. No one can ride a rollercoaster forever.

* * *

Finally Sera confided in Lois. Or tried to. Lois was still seeing Lionel from time to time but it was very different from Sera's relationship with Tarq. For one thing Lois seemed less invested in it. She had fallen hook, line and sinker for Lionel in terms of the bedroom but remained aware that he wasn't very reliable long term.

Sera envied Lois her sangfroid. She wished she could manage the same calm and collectedness.

"Tarq's been a bit strange recently," she began.

They were at Lois's house, an increasingly rare Saturday afternoon when the two of them were planning a night out as Tarq had been away for several days.

Lois drew a line of Chanel Rouge Noir polish down her nail. "I can't believe the hype over this stuff," she said, reviewing it. "My sister managed to get me this bottle through her work contacts but it's apparently like gold dust."

Sera peered at it. "It is very dark. Kind of gothic."

"It's supposed to look like dried blood. I think I'll put some glitter over the top of it."

This was probably sacrilege but as Lois got loads of designer cosmetic samples through her sister she was never very reverential about them.

Sera tried again. "I don't know what's up with Tarq. He seems distant, sometimes."

Lois blew up on the now glittery nail. "He's probably just stressed about Paris and everything. Sorting out his affairs."

"Paris?"

"You know, the job he's taken in Paris. He'll be busy with the preparations I should think."

A cold dread was creeping around Sera's heart. What Paris job? "He'll be in London next year."

Lois looked at her, frowning. "He's going to Paris, not London. He was offered some hugely prestigious artist-in-residence thing there. Didn't he tell you?" She saw from Sera's face that this was completely news to her. "God, Sera, I hope I haven't put my foot in it. Lionel mentioned it ages ago. I just assumed everyone knew."

Everyone did know, except Sera. "He hasn't told me." Her voice felt tight and miserable.

Lois looked guilty and uncomfortable. "There must be a reason. Maybe he's trying to figure out how often he could get back to see you. Or - " her face brightened " - maybe he was scared to tell you in case you didn't want a long distance relationship?"

Sera feared the opposite was a more likely scenario. Tarq wouldn't want to pursue a relationship in another country. She was quite confident she'd still want to date him if he went to live on Mars.

"I feel such an idiot. I don't know what to say," Lois was saying. "I just assumed that it was open knowledge."

Sera sat there, numb with misery.

"You'll have to ask him about it," Lois said.

There was no way Sera could do that. She was going to have to grit her teeth, keep up the pretence of not knowing, and steel herself for the inevitable "adieu" when Tarq had the good-while-it-lasted conversation.

If only she hadn't told her parents. They were going to think she was a fool and she could have saved them a world of stress.

32. Revelation

With all the uncertainty Sera was surprised when Tarq picked her up early on Saturday morning. "I thought we could spend the long weekend in London," he said. The following Monday was May Day, a bank holiday, so there was no school.

School was all over the place anyway now, just revision classes for the looming A-level exams. Sera had been working hard to distract herself from her ongoing anxieties over their relationship status and felt she could do with a break from her books.

Conversation felt superficial as they headed towards the capital. They spoke about other people - Joel, Jasper and Barry, Lois and Lionel - rather than themselves. The traffic wasn't too bad entering the outskirts of London but there seemed to be a lot of people heading out of the place. Next year that would probably be her, making weekend trips home.

At his place they climbed the stairs again and Tarq unlocked the door of his top floor apartment.

Sera walked through into the living room.

She stopped short.

There, on the wall where she was sure there had previously been a landscape, was Tarq's painting of her.

The painting that was supposed to be in Tokyo following the quarter of a million pound transaction. What was it doing here?

She turned to him, confused, momentarily wondering if it was a print or a replica.

He answered the question in her eyes. "I decided not to sell it."

"But all that money!"

He looked slightly cagey. "It's complicated. Both the buyer and Lionel knew I had no intention of selling it. Lionel certainly."

Sera was completely confused. "You mean it wasn't a real offer?"

"Yes, it was a real offer, but it kind of worked for all parties. The buyer owns a couple of my earlier works which shot up in value as a result of the publicity. Lionel got his publicity, and we all got rid of Victoria."

"So you didn't actually give up a quarter of a million pounds then?"

"I did. Once the hype started to happen he wanted it more than ever, even offered to raise his offer, but there's no way I would ever sell it. I don't want some other guy waking up to a naked painting of my girlfriend every day, of the future mother of my children."

What?!

Tarq continued. "The first painting anyway. I hope to paint you many more times in future. But the first one is special. It's mine." He stood there, regarding it.

Rewind rewind. Sera's brain was flipping out.

"What you just said..." She couldn't bring herself to repeat it, surely she must have misheard?

Tarq faced her. "About you being the mother of my children? In future, not immediately. And if you want to as well, of course."

Sera noted with some amusement that her wishes were the afterthought. "I'd have to think about it." She kept her face deadpan.

He was momentarily disconcerted. "Years away, I meant. If you still want to be with me then."

As if she could ever imagine a time when she wouldn't want to be with him. "Likewise."

Tarq put his hands on her shoulders, his eyes searing into hers. "My feelings won't ever change, Seraphina. But if you fall in love with someone else, I'll deal with it."

She felt both elated and weak. He kissed her and it felt like the kiss of life.

"I hadn't really thought that far ahead." She had to be honest with him. "I really do want to try and make a go of it as an artist. Study and graduate and everything. I've already started looking at accommodation for next year."

Once again he had that uneasy look on his face. This time Sera couldn't let it drop. "What's wrong? You say all this stuff and then you seem reluctant or evasive or something."

He took a breath. "It's not that. I've just been fighting with myself over something, because I know how selfish it is of me."

Sera tried to reassure him. "If you mean your job in France I already know about that. Lois let it slip."

She could see the surprise on his face. "It's related to that." He brushed the hair back from her face and tilted it towards him, tracing past her jaw.

"I want you to defer Saint Martins and come and live with me in Paris."

* * *

Give up university and live with Tarq in Paris?

The idea threw Sera for six. Images started flashing through her mind: the concern and anger of her parents, the Eiffel Tower, carrying her art satchel to Saint Martins, coffee in a Parisian café, enjoying a night in with as-yet-unknown housemates, walking along the Seine.

London Bridge. The Louvre. Trafalgar square. The Arc de Triomphe. The Tube. The Métro. The Tate. Montmartre.

Being with Tarq...

As soon as this last image passed into her mind she struggled to bring back London. The thought of being with him eclipsed everything else. She could barely hear what he was saying.

"It could be like a gap year. You could also take classes in Paris if you wanted to. Even switch to a school there. I'll fully support you, financially and with whatever else."

It was too much to take in. But she knew he needed an answer now. "There are some conditions."

She saw hope flare in his gaze. Coming from someone so strong and always so reserved, it was moving. But his voice remained calm.

"Name them."

"I pay my own way. I'll get a job waiting tables, sweeping floors, whatever. I'm not going to live off you." If she started doing that it might get hard to stop. Sera wanted to forge her own way and establish her own career. She didn't want to be an expensive leech like Victoria.

His relief and joy were palpable. "You could earn a week's wages sketching for a couple of hours in Montmartre. Your speed and skill are easily sufficient."

"Your classes helped with that."

Tarq brought his lips down on her again. "I have so much more to teach you." As he deepened the embrace Sera was aware he was talking about other, more intimate subjects than art.

Then he drew back. "You know I'm too old and world-worn for you, don't you? That I'll probably end up making you miserable?"

"Miserably happy."

"It won't always be easy, Sera. When I get into my art, sometimes... it takes over. Nothing else exists."

He was trying to put up barriers now, anxious that she was making an informed decision.

"So if you were in the flow and I came up to you and did this..." Sera unbuttoned her blouse slowly "...you wouldn't be distracted?"

The glint of heat was already in his eye again. "I can't tell. Possibly not. Maybe if you continued a little further..."

Sera opened the blouse entirely and then reached down to her waistband, hesitating there.

"Lower." The tone of command was back in his voice.

She slipped her jeans off.

"More."

Now she challenged him. "Not until you tell me why."

"Why what?"

"Why you want me with you?"

Tarq scowled, frustrated. "You know why. Now remove those."

Sera wasn't going to give him the striptease he wanted until she got her answer. "You've never said why." He had never said those words. And she wanted to hear them.

"I've never told you? I suppose I've thought it so many times in my mind that I assumed I had done." He took her hands and looked at her, tenderness mingled with ardour. "I love you, Seraphina. I want you to be with me always. I started falling in love with you from the moment you disrobed in my class to the point where I realised you were the one for me. The only one."

"You took your time making it known," Sera said.

"I know. I fought it for ages as it seemed wrong and I was determined not to give anyone else the chance to screw up my life again. I haven't let anyone get close to me for years. But you got under my skin. The more time I spent with you it became about so much more than sexual attraction. You are intelligent, beautiful, unbelievably talented. When you were with me in hospital that day I knew I wanted you by my side, permanently. That I needed you to be part of my life and my future."

It was the most sincere and eloquent Tarq had ever been. His words made her heart sing and her body long to be possessed by him.

"I love you too." She did. With all her heart.

Sera slipped off the rest of her clothes and stood there, once again naked, before him. Any artistic appreciation of her form was at that moment drowned out by raw, sheer lust.

To tease him further she ran her hands over her own body, cupping her breasts, slipping her hand down and between. She loved watching his reaction.

It had more than the desired effect. With a primal urge he grabbed her, carried her to the bedroom and threw her on the bed. Replaced her hands with his own. Devoured her body. Was relentless with her for over an hour.

She lay there afterwards bathed in his warmth and his love. "You're probably going to regret asking me to Paris."

Tarq was confused. "Why?"

"You may not get much work done if that is anything to go by." She had every intention of distracting him on a daily basis, if the past hour was the result.

"It's a risk I'm more than willing to take." He looked deep into her eyes and she saw not only love and desire but also respect in his gaze.

"Your talent may one day belong to the world, Seraphina, but you belong to me. Always."

184

33. Epilogue

Five years later

"Trista Regina" - "the Sad Queen" - a leading art critic had dubbed it, and the name stuck.

Sera had never thought to give a specific title to the portrait. She was overwhelmed enough with painting such a momentous subject and trying to do some kind of justice to the honour of the commission.

She also hadn't meant to make it sad. But the eyes she had painted were the eyes of someone who had lived a very long time, who had seen eras of history rise and fall. Someone who had lived through war and huge change and love and bereavement and the passing of a millennium.

"It's more nostalgic than sad," Tarq had said. "But it is sad."

The portrait was universally acclaimed though it caused some controversy. A cartoonist in one of the newspapers drew a pastiche of it, titled "Miserable Monarch", linking it to a recent royal scandal.

Most importantly, the subject herself was apparently "delighted" with the final painting. "She has said, though this is strictly off the record," a courtier told Sera, "that it is by far her favourite."

Given how often the famous lady had been painted this was high praise from the highest source.

The past five years had gone by in such a whirl that Sera had barely had time to stop and breathe. She had moved to Paris and ended up giving up her place at St Martin's to instead go to the École Nationale Supérieure des Beaux-Arts by the Seine. Paris suited her.

She had somehow fallen in with a bohemian set of artists and socialites and one day ended up painting a girl who was a well-known model.

"*Honnête mais gentil*," was the verdict - "honest but kind" - and suddenly Sera was in vogue and in demand.

It led to a flurry of commissions from bright young Parisians wanting portraits, and Sera's work became commanded higher up the social scale until she painted an elderly duchess, a distant cousin of England's monarch.

Which had led to the ultimate commission. Sera was one of the youngest artists to ever be awarded such a recognition and she made the most of it.

Tarq was there at her side, throughout. She couldn't have managed it without his support and guidance.

They were sitting by the window of their Paris apartment eating breakfast and looking at the newspaper coverage of the portrait which had finally been unveiled by the National Portrait Gallery. The previous two days had been a non-stop whirl of interviews for Sera, and she had flown back to France the previous night.

"You look very tired," he told her. "Beautiful, but exhausted."

"That was due to you, not the press," Sera told him. He had been relentless with her in bed the past night, both of them hyped up with the success of Sera's royal portrait.

"You usually have plenty of stamina." There was a glint in his eye and Sera took it for the challenge that it was.

She let her robe fall to her waist. She wore nothing under it. Even though Tarq had painted her a dozen or more times over the past years, sometimes clothed and sometimes nude, he still reacted instantly if she spontaneously disrobed before him.

As she had anticipated he caught his breath. "Already?" he asked.

"Always ready."

He swept her up and carried her to their bed, where he made love to her slowly and tenderly, drawing it out and making her beg him to give her release. Between the sheets he still had absolute command and control of her body.

Tarq gazed down into her eyes. "I love you beyond words, Seraphina."

Afterwards she lay there with him in a warm and blissful state. "So what's next?" he asked her.

"A holiday. A long, long holiday." Friends of theirs owned a chateau on the Loire and Sera planned to escape there for a couple of months. It was early summer and the perfect time to get out of Paris, before it became hot and crowded with tourists. She had a vague dream of buying fresh produce from local *marchés* and working her way through Larousse. And doing another portrait of Tarq, whom she never got tired of painting.

It was easy for Tarq to get away as well when he wanted to. His work remained in high demand, both due to his talent and Lionel's continued astute business management. Last year he had got Tarq to paint a series of seascapes featuring Chinese boats that had sold for an absolute fortune to buyers in Hong Kong and the Chinese mainland.

"We should hold a massive party this summer and get everyone over," Sera suggested. She had missed seeing her friends over the past months due to the intense work on the portrait and how busy they both were.

Since graduating Joel had rapidly established himself as a leading costume designer in London's West End, working on many major musicals.

Lois, who had failed all her A-levels and not bothered to re-sit them, was flitting around France having forged a bizarrely successful career for herself as a kind of neo-burlesque performer, doing everything from singing to stand-up. She spoke fluent French with the most atrocious accent possible but people seemed to find it amusing and endearing.

Lionel still pined after her but Lois still considered him too much of a flake and had no intention of settling down yet.

Victoria, whose ex-husband Maurice still did business with Lionel, had married an elderly Texan billionaire and was long gone out of everyone's lives.

"A party? That won't be very relaxing. I'd prefer to have you all to myself," Tarq told Sera, tracing his fingers over her stomach and making her skin tauten and tingle.

"It will just be one weekend."

He rolled over to face her. "I had another project in mind," he told her.

"Oh?" Sera initially assumed it was something to do with painting.

But he ran his hand up her thighs, moving her legs apart for him again. "Getting you pregnant. Or at least practising doing so."

Sera felt a jolt in her stomach. "You want to start a family?"

"If you're ready."

Was she ready? Lionel would probably kill her, he was already working on a huge and prestigious list of commissions. They included a former American president as well as a couple of A-list Hollywood celebrities. "Strike while the iron's hot," Lionel had said. "Once you've done a couple more this high profile, you'll be set for life."

It was a lot to take in. It would mean a lot of travel, big money and big expectations.

Still there was no reason she couldn't paint and have children. It wasn't as though she needed to work out of an office every day. They could always get a nanny to help out.

Thinking these things, Sera came to a decision. "Okay."

"Just like that?"

"Just like that." She smiled, and reached up to pull him down to kiss her. The thought of having sex with him and trying to get pregnant gave the whole act an extra erotic edge.

As he plunged into her she felt owned by him and knew that she owned him likewise. They were one.

Before long they would have tangible proof of this, the purest and most binding symbol of their love. And this time it would not be a creation of Art, but of Nature.

About Noël Cades

Noël Cades is a British writer who currently lives in Sydney, Australia. A fan of romance from historic to erotic, some of Noël's favourite authors include Jilly Cooper, Jackie Collins, Elizabeth Rolls, Violet Winspear and Victoria Holt.

Noël is always delighted to hear from other fans, readers and writers of romance.

You can contact Noël at **noelcades@gmail.com**

Noël's website is at **http://www.noelcades.com**

Visit Noël's blog to sign up for exclusive news and the chance to receive new free book giveaways.

Excerpts from *Summer's Edge* by **Noël Cades**

Alice remained silent throughout this. She was still feeling disappointed and uncertain. She tried to tell herself it was for the best. Really, she should be grateful that he had just decided to move past it.

But she still felt embarrassed. She picked at the grass next to her, pulling off a small flower, avoiding looking at the play.

Then a shadow fell over them. She looked up.

It was Mr Walker.

"I want a word with you. In the pavilion, now," he ordered her. His eyes pierced into hers and he looked furious.

Numb, she obeyed, walking ahead of him.

Inside it was empty and he closed the door behind them and turned to her.

"What the fuck do you think you're playing at?"

He was absolutely incensed. He stood there, suddenly the adult, the authority, not just some guy she had kissed in a pub.

Someone she had compromised. Alice couldn't think of anything to say.

She stood there in front of him. His scent of faint cologne and sun-warmed skin was disturbingly familiar to her, mingling with the dusty wood and sports equipment smell of the pavilion.

"Did you know who I was?" he asked.

"Yes." There didn't seem to be any point in lying.

He glared at her and she looked back at him. His eyes pierced into her, their light grey-blue contrasting with his tanned complexion. He was one of the most devastatingly attractive men she had ever seen. All the more so now as his anger turned his face into carved steel.

As terrified and awkward as Alice felt, she also felt slightly defiant. After all she hadn't done anything wrong or illegal.

Then suddenly he grasped her by the shoulders and brought his mouth down on hers, hard. Surprised, she initially squirmed to escape his grasp then yielded as her forced his tongue into her mouth. His lips were bruising hers, he was almost biting her yet she wanted more.

Her hands, which had pushed against his chest to try and get away, went round his neck and she arched against him.

He was trying to hurt her, devour her. Punish her. All at once. But he wanted her too. She could taste his need, raw and urgent. Feel the hotness of his breath as he nearly suffocated her with his kiss.

His mouth left hers and moved to her neck, half embracing, half biting it. She tasted blood on her lip where he had crushed it with his own. He was gripping her hard and she clung to him. She didn't even care that he was hurting her.

He could have ripped all her clothes off right there and forced himself upon her. She had never wanted anyone so much.

Then just as suddenly he thrust her away from him. He swore under his breath as he tried to recover himself.

"Is that what you wanted?"

"No... yes... I mean..." Alice had no idea what to say. She was shaken and half in misery, half in ecstasy.

His face was like granite, its angles unyielding.

"Get out and don't come back here again. Stay out of my way," he said.

* * *

Alice tried to enjoy herself at the barbecue but she couldn't relax with Mr Walker just metres away, deliberately avoiding her. She had no appetite but knew she needed to eat something to avoid getting completely drunk on an empty stomach.

Graeme was good company and buoyed up by misery, alcohol and perhaps a desire to make a point to Mr Walker she flirted with him a bit. He was the kind of guy you could flirt with without it meaning much. Besides she knew he preferred Jules. She also noticed that Mr Walker's gaze was frequently on her and he didn't look happy about her flirting with Graeme. Or she hoped that was why he looked annoyed.

As the beer went down the revelry increased and someone accidentally knocked a glass full of beer over Alice. It went all over her top.

Feeling as though nothing much more could go wrong with the day she found her way to the kitchen and tried to sponge out the worst at the sink. If the beer dried on it, it would smell awful and probably stain the fabric. Hopefully even though she was getting her top even more wet it would dry quickly in the sun.

As she was finishing getting the worst off someone else came into the kitchen. She knew even before she turned that it was Mr Walker. He looked angry.

"Did you come here deliberately?" he asked.

She faced him. "I came here with Becky. I didn't know you'd be here. Or care," she added.

"What have you done to your shirt?"

"Someone spilt beer on it. I was washing it off."

"You can't go back out like that. You look like a wet t-shirt competition," he told her.

Alice looked down and went red. The wet fabric had gone transparent and soaked through her bra too.

Without a word Mr Walker pulled off his own shirt and handed it to her. He wore nothing under it. Alice was transfixed by his physique. His arms rippled with muscle and his flat, hard chest was tanned a deep gold. He was far fitter than she expected a cricketer to be, really powerful looking.

"Put this on."

194

The shirt was white cotton and warm from his body. She held it. It smelt of him. She wanted to envelop herself in it but she didn't follow his order.

"You want me to walk out of here wearing your shirt with you following me, topless?" she asked him.

He was silent for a moment, glaring at her. She was right, it would have exactly the opposite effect he intended. The situation was bad enough as it was.

"I don't want them gawping at you."

Alice's stomach gave a secret flip. Possessive and protective. He clearly didn't feel as neutrally towards her as he wanted to.

"The sun will dry it. I'll cross my arms." As she said this, she deliberately left her arms uncrossed and put her shoulders back slightly.

It had the desired effect. He was momentarily transfixed.

"Jesus Christ."

Alice took charge of the situation. "You should put this back on." Instead of just handing it to him she went to put it over his head meaning her arms were raised and her body was nearly against his. He was still for a second before taking a step backwards. A muscle clenched in his jaw.

"Just give me the shirt." She did so and he put it back on.

Then they both stood there. The tension was unbearable. She knew he wanted her and was fighting against it with every fibre of his being.

She broke the ice. "I am sorry you know. We were all just having fun the other night and I just didn't think about the implications."

"You were just messing around with me because I'm employed at your school?"

"God no, that wasn't why." Alice couldn't believe he thought this. Surely he'd realised how much she also wanted him to kiss her that night?

"So even if I hadn't been, you would have still put on your little act?" he asked.

What act? "I wasn't acting, I genuinely..."

"You wanted it too?"

"Yes." It was barely a whisper.

For a moment she thought he was going to kiss her again. He was wavering. Then he stood straighter. "I'm way too old for you, Alice, and I work at your school. Get back outside."

To find out what happens between Alice and Mr Walker, get Noël Cades' thrilling taboo student-teacher romance, Summer's Edge.